BLOKES IN THE HOUSE

THREE OLD MEN GO INTO LOCKDOWN

WINDY MOUNTAIN
BOOK 5

JOHN MARTIN

CONTENTS

ONE
THE PANDEMIC HITS HOME
2020

THE OLD MAN looked up when someone burst through the door of the hospital room.

A sturdy woman wearing a starched white dress marched towards his bed clutching a clipboard.

Sister Daisy Rowbottom glared down at him. "I heard you were in here, James. How was your trip to Ireland?" She nodded towards his daughter, who was sitting in a blue vinyl chair on the other side of the bed. "Morning, Maddie."

James Northan often bumped into Daisy in the aisles of Roses Supermarket. She had earned a reputation as a dragon before she retired from nursing some years ago, but she had mellowed. These days she liked a chat by the frozen peas.

But what was she doing here looking so fearsome again? She had to be well into her seventies. How had she even been able to squeeze into that dress! Her white cap emblazoned with its red cross looked like something she had brought back from a field hospital in the Crimean War.

"Oh, I get it." James stretched back on his pillows, adjusted one of his hearing aids, then put his hand behind him to cradle his head. "You are on your way to a fancy dress party." He smiled. "Let me guess what as? Florence Nightingale? Have you considered taking a lamp along as a prop?"

Daisy's eyes became slits. "This is no time for frivolity, James. I volunteered when they put out a call for trained nurses to help get them through this COVID crisis."

James rolled his eyes. "Oh, not someone else over-reacting!"

Daisy looked down at the clipboard. "Right," she said. "We need to determine who needs to be here and who needs to be discharged."

James wriggled himself further up on his pillows and made a Victory sign with two fingers. "Did you hear that, Maddie? They are letting me go home." He turned his head the other way. "I have had a bit of cardiac trouble, Daisy. But I am tickety-boo now."

"That's not what it says here." Daisy tapped the clipboard with a chubby index finger. "You're lucky a bystander knew how to administer the kiss of life. Otherwise you'd still be dead."

James's smile disappeared. "Reprobates like Moose should not be allowed to learn CPR!"

Daisy spotted the dried blood on the back of James's liver-spotted hand where the cannula had been inserted, and scowled. "Who did that?"

She didn't wait for an answer. "I can see standards have slipped around here." She cleared her throat. "We shall have to do something about that."

Daisy looked down at the clipboard again. "I see this is your third time in Windy Mountain Hospital, James." She read on, looked up and screeched. "What were you thinking checking yourself out? At your age?"

"I am only 82!" he shouted back.

James took a deep breath and lowered his voice. "As I said, I am fine now. Angioplasty worked wonders on me."

"They wouldn't have transferred you back here if they didn't think you needed further bed-rest."

"Bed-rest? You are joking! I had proper bed-rest in Hobart. I had a single room in a private hospital, with good food and doctors who speak English." James's left hand was tethered to an IV machine and it hurt every time he tugged it, but he was able to wave his free fist towards the other bed. "Here I am forced to share."

Daisy looked at the smooth light-blue quilt and the clean, white pillows, then looked back blankly. "No one is even occupying that bed."

"Maybe not. But it is a constant reminder that at any time someone might be wheeled in here in the middle of the night. That is when things happen in this hick hospital. I did not have sleep apnea until I came in here. Now I wake up every 10 minutes with the noise at night."

"Oh, James!"

"Do they not know who I *was*! Who Maddie *is*! The great unwashed should look up to more important individuals who rise to the exalted position of mayor."

"Public hospitals don't play favourites."

"I paid taxes all my life. For what? The food here is disgusting. In Hobart, dinner came with a little bottle of wine. Now I cannot even get a decent cup of tea."

Daisy forced a smile. "I think you're exaggerating, James."

"Am I? Is it any wonder I checked myself out? I would still be recuperating in the tranquility of my own cottage and in the comfort of my own soft bed, if it had not been for those clowns."

"Clowns?" Daisy frowned.

"Bert Whish-Willson and Clarence Noodle had the audacity to visit me."

"I thought you were friends with Wish-Wash and Oodles."

"Just because we sometimes used to sit together on the bench on the High Street does not mean we are kindred spirits." He sounded like a deflating balloon as his breath started running out. "You will find this out soon. The older you get, the more you are forced to mix with whoever is left."

"But didn't you go to Ireland with them?"

"Mistake of my life!" James looked towards the ceiling. "After the way they treated me on that trip, I cannot fathom how they had the bareface cheek to come to my cottage where I was recuperating after my release from this poor excuse for a hospital. Who gives a man flowers, for heaven's sake? To add insult to injury, they picked them from my own garden." He breathed in, then exhaled just as noisily. "And who gives a bottle of Raki to a man who is convalescing unless they are trying to finish him off?"

Daisy spoke slowly. "I'm afraid I don't actually know what Raki is." She glanced at Maddie in search of a clue.

"No use looking at her. Maddie has never been to Crete. Raki is a crude alcoholic drink distilled for a certain clientele. Mainly peasants! You would know it if you smelled it. They probably market it in this country as hospital disinfectant."

The nasty taste in his mouth intensified just thinking about it. "The final straw was when they tried to wind me up by claiming my so-called Irish cousin was on his way to Australia. I showed them the door quick smart, I can tell you."

Daisy glanced down at her clipboard again and flipped over the page. "That's when you had your second collapse?"

James tried to rearrange a pillow by reaching behind with his untethered hand. Maddie reacted to his grunt of frustration by getting to her feet, and sliding the pillow behind his back. But he didn't thank her, preferring to keep up his tirade towards Daisy. "Can you blame me? I was supposed to be keeping my blood pressure down."

Daisy kept looking at Dr Rashidmanhi's notes. "You know, not everyone actually makes it to the Windy Mountain Hospital in the back of that ambulance. Some have to finish their trip in the back of a roadside assistance truck."

James shook his fist. "That ambulance was state of the art when we bought it. I should know. I was chairman of the hospital board in those days."

"You'd know it was an ice-cream van in its former life then?" Daisy said. "Why do you think they were happy to get rid of it? It's not good for business when your ice-cream van keeps breaking down and the soft-serve all melts."

"I'm here, am I not?"

Daisy shuffled to the end of the bed and hung the clipboard on the rail. "You're right. You are here. We'll just have to make the best of it." She sighed. "I can see you've had a bad run, too. We all know what stress Messerschmitt caused you, now these health issues beset you."

In the next breath, she said: "You won't mind if we put someone else in this room? We might even have to squeeze a third bed in if things get really bad."

"Over my dead body!" James's eyes strained against their sockets. "I'm not sharing my room with riff-raff."

"You won't have a choice if it gets as bad as we're expecting."

"In that case, I *demand* to go home."

"I think not," Daisy said, lifting her chins. "You're what we call an essential patient."

"People were right about you," James hissed. "You are nothing but a bossy old spinster who likes to control your patient's lives."

Daisy's eyes darkened. For a long time, she said nothing. Then she said slowly: "You *will* tell me if you can't move your bowels, Mr Northan. Perhaps the nurse who butchered the insertion of your cannula also needs to practise doing enemas."

———

He watched her stride out of the room, then locked eyes with Maddie. "That is it. I'm checking myself out again."

"Is that a good idea, Daddy? You know what happened last time."

"I would have been fine if those fools had not come visiting."

"I'm sure they meant the best."

"This time I will put a padlock on the gate."

Maddie gave an exasperated sigh. "The doctors have only just got your blood pressure back under control. You heard Daisy. They won't let you check out so easily this time."

"I am not — I emphasise *not* — sharing my room with sick people. Besides, you heard her. She has become a tyrant again."

"You just hate being outbullied, Daddy!"

"What's that supposed to mean? At least I have the courtesy to listen to people before telling them what to do."

Maddie rolled her eyes.

James rotated his hand to show the dried blood. "Daisy really could not care less an incompetent nurse has used me as a darts board. She just wants to resume her reign of terror."

"Oh Daddy."

"Do not *Daddy* me. She could easily organise a line-up of nurses so I could identify the culprit. But no, she would rather humiliate the lot of them to show them who is boss."

James sighed heavily. "That is how she operates. You heard her threaten me with an enema."

Maddie gave a little laugh. "I think you'll find she was only joking."

"People thought it was a medical miracle the day she retired, and patients' stress levels all dropped."

———

Maddie steepled her fingers and squeezed her eyes shut. "I didn't want to have to tell you this, Daddy . . ."

"Tell me what?"

"You *can't* go home."

James opened his eyes wide, so wide it hurt. "Why not?"

Maddie opened her eyes. "I didn't think you'd mind. He said he had no where else to stay."

James tugged at a strand of his straggly, thin hair. "Who?"

"Your cousin."

"My cousin? Which cousin?"

"Your cousin from Ireland."

"Conn? I thought Bert and Clarence were just trying to wind me up." He stared into space. "Where does a bog Irishman like that even get the money to travel?"

"He arrived two days ago," Maddie said. "The State Government insists that all new arrivals to the state self-isolate for 14 days."

James buried his head in his free hand, and hissed: "You let him infect my cottage!"

"If your nephew hadn't burnt down the hotel . . . "

James looked up. "At least you know for sure Messerschmitt *is* your cousin. You do not know the Irishman from Adam. What were you thinking inviting him to stay?"

"I could hardly tell him to go sleep under the bridge. How would that look? I have an election coming up. Remember?"

"What about a hotel in another town? Is it not about time Sltutz Plains took a share of Irish people?"

"He's flesh and blood."

"The jury is out on that. All we know for sure is his DNA matches the DNA found on my toothbrush. Bert Whish-Willson is not too fussy about which toothbrush he uses."

"But the Irishman's last name is Northan. You don't think that's a hint?"

"I don't think it is conclusive, no."

"I thought you'd be fine with it, especially seeing as you'd be in here for at least another two weeks."

"Is he showing symptoms of actually being sick?"

Maddie shrugged. "He's not answering my phone calls, or the door."

James banged his fist down on the bed. "Just what I need? A corpse in my cottage!"

"He can't be dead, Daddy. We can see the lights going on and off from our house."

"So you are letting him run up my electricity bills?" He rolled his eyes. "Great!"

Maddie folded her arms. "You can't go there now. If you insist on checking out of here, I'll just have to make other arrangements."

TWO
THE PENNY DROPS

JAMES WAS PACING up and down the foyer when Maddie walked into the hospital the next morning. He was dressed in the same creased suit he had been wearing when they had brought him in, and was holding an overnight bag.

The bag carried his pyjamas, a change of underwear and his toiletries, plus his take-home medications.

"I have been waiting for you for an hour. Why are you late?"

"I told you. I had to make arrangements." Maddie picked up his bag and turned towards the automatic glass doors, with James in tow.

"What is wrong with me staying in the big house with you?"

She turned her head. "It's cramped enough with Norm and I, Vicki and Velda and two cats."

"You would hardly know I was there."

Maddie stopped, put down the bag, and turned. "I'm sure you'll be very comfortable with the arrangements I've made for you. And it's only for three months."

"Three months? Did you just say three months!"

Maddie wrapped her arms around her torso. "That's the period of isolation health officials are recommending for people your age. The elderly are high risk. And I have a responsibility as mayor to insist on it. No exceptions."

"Three whole months?"

"The time will whizz by, Daddy."

"You get less incarceration time for murder!"

"Katy says she will leave food and supplies on the doorstep every day. That way, you'll never even have to leave the house."

"Katy?"

"Katy McDonnell."

"Good grief! She's married to Jerome O'Fury."

"So?"

The blood that had rushed to his face now drained from his head. "So O'Fury is a friend of Clarence's." He closed his eyes and put a hand to his forehead.

THREE
THE PENNY DROPS FURTHER

THE DRIVE to Oodles's place was over in minutes. The green weatherboard house sat at the top of a cul-de-sac on the hill.

"They're expecting you." Maddie kept the engine running by the kerb. "I obviously can't go to the door with you."

"They?" James looked out the passenger window towards the house, and his voice faltered. "W-who else is there?"

"I assumed you knew. We need to keep the oldest three people in town safe. Bert Wish-Willson is part of the fabric of Windy Mountain."

James swallowed, and hissed. "This is your idea of payback, is it not?"

"Payback?" Maddie looked at him. "For what?"

"For me sending you off to boarding school."

Maddie stared into the middle-distance. "I had forgotten about that. Those Church of England nuns sure were strict. You would have thought they'd have gone easier on an eight-year-old girl."

"It toughened you up."

"Is that what you think I'm trying to do to you?"

James looked towards the house again. So it had come to this?

Oodles had once answered to his every whim but the 85-year-old former council works supervisor refused to look up to him these days.

As for that big, fat oaf Wish-Wash, he had once been the town drunk. Goodness knows how he had even made it to 83!

Until recently, they had been the unlikely co-owners of the Windy Mountain Tasmanian Tiger Museum. James could have told them how that was likely to end!

"You know those old men still call me the Mayor?" James said.

"So? It just means they look up to you. You were mayor for a lot of years. I'd call that a mark of respect."

"Respect? Poppycock! They know you are the Mayor now. It's discourteous, that's what it is."

Maddie kissed him on the cheek. "It's only for three months. We can talk on the phone every day."

"How can you?" James said. "Don't you remember? Clarence had his phone disconnected when he had problems with those scammers?"

Maddie clicked her fingers. "I'll get Tom to organise it to be connected again. I'll ring you every day, I promise." She paused. "That's more than you did for me when I was an eight-year-old boarder."

James screwed up his face. "I made sure you had everything you needed. You never went without."

"Thanks for that, Daddy. And don't worry: we'll keep you well supplied, too."

James looked out the passenger window. "Just look at that house. It is not just common, it is tiny. Do you think we will all fit?"

"I'm told it has three bedrooms."

"It was simply demoralising when we had to share accommodation in Ireland. No one should ever be expected to see Bert naked. It was like being in the same room as a bull walrus."

"Oh Daddy!"

"Three months? And why? It's a big over-reaction to something that will surely blow over soon."

"It's not going to blow over."

"The trouble is this younger generation just cannot handle a bit of a sniffle."

"Oh, Daddy. It's much worse than that. Haven't you been watching the news?"

"Have you ever try to watch TV in hospital? The programs are sandwiched by funeral insurance adverts. Hospital patients are their target market."

Maddie shifted in her seat. "Can't you see I'm just trying to keep you safe?"

"You will bring my laptop?"

Maddie frowned. "Where is it?"

"In a drawer in the study. I can tell you where the key is."

"Fat lot of good that will do me when your cousin isn't answering the door."

James took hold of the handles on his overnight bag, tucked the plastic bag under his arm and started opening the passenger door. "I suppose that rules out my smart phone, too?"

Crow's feet formed at the side of Maddie's eyes. "You're not carrying it?"

"I think the medics were too busy trying to find my pulse to look for my phone."

Maddie tapped her head three times on the steering wheel. "I'd buy you a new one, but I can't think where. There's nowhere to buy them in Windy Mountain and we've been told not to travel out of town unless it's absolutely necessary."

"Can you not tell them we are important people?"

Maddie opened her eyes and shook her head slowly. "I don't think that would wash with health authorities, Daddy."

"That reminds me." James looked down at the chest of his shirt. "I have only got the clothes I am wearing and one change of underwear."

Maddie smiled. "And your pyjamas."

"They are going to be pretty stinky after three months."

"I'm sure Oodles has a washing machine."

James got out of the car, holding his bag, and turned around to stoop into the cabin. "It is probably a twin tub with a mangle. You think I want to do my washing in his ancient washing machine? No telling what I would catch."

"We know what you might catch if you don't go into isolation."

"The day will come when you young people will regret you acted so foolishly." James went to slam the door but stopped. "What about all the prescription meds they gave me?"

"What about them?"

"I've only got enough for a month."

"It's not a problem. I'll get your GP to prescribe some more."

"How will he know what I need? They have put me on a raft of medication." It astounded him. A few years ago, the only thing he had to remember each day was to put his hearing aids in. Now he had a multitude of pills he was supposed to swallow after breakfast, and even more to remember to take before bed.

"The hospital would have sent the list to Doc Jenkins. Do you want them in a Webster-pak?"

"A what?"

"A medicine pack so you know what tablets to take when?"

He had that nasty taste back in his mouth. "I'm not senile!"

He slammed the car door shut.

FOUR
YOUR ROOM, SIR

With one hand sliding up the safety rail, he awkwardly ascended the small flight of steps at the end of the path with his overnight bag, which felt like a school bag.

The door opened ahead of him.

"Welcome, old mate." Oodles ushered him into the spartan hallway. Clarence was not using his walking stick. He was *supposed* to be using it all the time. Did Dr Jenkins know he was disobeying him?

Wish-Wash put his foot out to stop the front door from closing, then poked his head out and surveyed the front yard.

James swung around and groaned. "Who else are you expecting?"

Wish-Wash turned to face him. "You might have been followed, Jimbo."

"By whom?"

"By Messerschmitt."

James's voice dropped. "Oh, very droll, Bert. You know as well as I do he is languishing in a jail awaiting trial. We will not be seeing him again for many, many years."

Wish-Wash closed the door, and broke into a smile, which showed his bad teeth. "You didn't really mean that, did you?"

James looked him in the eye. "Did not mean what?"

"That you didn't want to see us ever again? Because it looks like you'll be seeing us all day, every day for the next three months."

James dropped his overnight bag, making a thump on the wooden floorboards, and wrinkled his nose as he looked around.

The hall smelled of bleach. James knew what Oodles was like. Not only was he ridiculously practical, he had always maintained a spotless workshop when he worked at the council.

Oodles looked down at the bag on the floor. "Is that all of your luggage, old son?"

"I have come straight from the hospital, but I'm hoping Maddie will be able to gather some more things for me."

"Not too much, I hope." Oodles looked at Wish-Wash. "I don't know where we'd put it."

"No need to worry. I will contain it all to my own room."

Oodles rubbed the back of his neck. James had seen him do that before, and he sensed there was something he needed to say.

"Maddie says there are three bedrooms here?" James said slowly.

Oodles now rubbed his temple. "Technically, yes."

"Technically?"

"I actually use the third bedroom as a storeroom of sorts."

"Of sorts?"

"I couldn't even tell you what's in there. I never go in, even to clean. It was always Madge's place of retreat."

Wish-Wash flashed another big grin as he pointed to the bag. "No servants here, Jimbo. Grab that, and I'll show you to our room."

James trudged behind him down the hall, past a black phone connected to a curly cord and sitting in a cradle set in the wall.

The room they veered into had two single beds, which were arranged in an L-shape along separate walls. Wish-Wash's was nearest to the door. At the foot, a tower of large red leather-bound books grew like the Leaning Tower of Pisa from the solitary bedside table.

Wish-Wash pointed to the built-in wardrobe. "You'll find a bit of space left for your clothes. If Maddie brings more, you can always bung them in Oodles's wardrobe. Now Madge is gone, he doesn't need all that storage space in the master bedroom. He really only needs that room so he's nearer to the dunny on account of his Woolworths bladder."

James sat down on his bed and threw his head in his hands.

Why was this happening?

Normally a mayor and a town drunk were unlikely even to meet, but that all changed when Wish-Wash claimed in 1967 he had been awakened in a bus shelter by a Tasmanian Tiger whose breath smelled of apples that he said came from the orchard James owned.

The newspapers and TV reported his every word to a gullible public.

The Tasmanian Tiger was finally declared extinct in the 1990s but the last one in captivity had died in a Hobart zoo in 1936. So the chances of a dead animal strolling down the main street of Windy Mountain in 1967 were even slighter than its chances of hailing a No. 2 bus at that time of the morning.

James had felt justified putting an end to the nonsense.

Wish-Wash had never forgiven him for what he did.

Now he never missed the opportunity to get one back.

———

When James had recovered his equilibrium, he got up from the bed and walked over to the tower of books and picked up the one on top of the stack.

It was an encyclopaedia, and the embossed gold lettering on the spine told him it was everything to do with the letters 'Q-R-S'.

James flicked through some pages. "I thought you only read sci-fi books?"

"I had read them all," Wish-Wash said.

James looked up sharply. "You cannot have read them all! Sci-fi is about the future, man. They are still being written!"

"Pffft. What do modern sci-fi writers know about the future? Give me Jules Verne any day." Wish-Wash patted the next book on the stack, making it wobble. "The problem is he's not writing any new books, so I traded in my sci-fi collection for these babies. Bet you didn't know the Slutz Plains Op Shop traded books, too?"

James turned to the front of the book, then prodded the page with an index finger. "It says here that this set of encyclopaedias was printed in 1963. That makes them middle-aged."

"What's that got to do with the price of eggs?" Wish-Wash caressed the top book again. "Knowledge doesn't change."

"I think you will find it does," James said. "You have gone from one extreme to the other: the nonsense of the future to the irrelevance of the past." He snapped the book shut. "When this set of books was printed, Britain still ruled the globe. I bet the world map in this thing is coloured with lots of pink."

"Ah, that's where you're wrong," Wish-Wash said. " If you bothered to look, smartarse, you'd see I don't have the letter 'M'. I didn't get the volume with all the maps."

James frowned. "The set is not even complete then?"

"So? Books go astray." Wish-Wash smirked. "I held back one of my Jules Vernes in retaliation." He pointed to the wardrobe. "I hid it in the dark where they'll never find it."

James returned his book carefully to the top of the pile. "Oh, very droll, Bert. Can you not see you have been had? Google is the new font of all knowledge."

Wish-Wash banged a hand on the top book, making the tower wobble some more. "You're just jealous, Jimbo, I'll be spending the next three months enriching my mind. You'll be amazed what I'm going to find in these books."

———

When the other old men gave him a guided tour of the house, James was pleased to see a TV in the living room.

But it had a tiny screen encased in a large cabinet in the corner of the room.

"Does that old thing even work?" he asked.

"No reason why it wouldn't, old cock," Oodles said. "It went like the clappers the one time we turned it on."

"Once?" James rolled his eyes. "Let me guess? You watched the Coronation in black and white?"

"Get away with you! Did we even have TV coverage in 1953? No, this was on July 21, 1969. Madge and I watched Neil Armstrong step on to the moon."

"And you haven't watched anything since?"

"Has there been anything worth watching since?"

———

Rooming with Wish-Wash went from difficult to unbearable.

The wardrobe rack was mostly full of Wish-Wash's second-hand clothes he had bought from the Opportunity Shop. But he rationed himself to his elastic-banded pants and three loud shirts, which infuriated James, who barely had enough room for his one suit.

Wish-Wash solved that problem when he spilled a cup of cream soup right down the back of James's woollen suit.

Katy took it away for dry-cleaning and James had to borrow a pair of Oodles's overalls to wear each day. These were splattered with hard, dry green spots of paint.

Wish-Wash also had an aversion to fresh air coming in the room.

"It is so stuffy in here, can we not open the window?" James asked, night after night.

"You must be flamin' joking. It's freezing out there."

FIVE
SCRABBLE RABBLE
12 DAYS IN

As James studied the board, the only noise in the room was the ticking of the walnut-wood clock on the mantelpiece.

He would have preferred to have been marshalling chess pieces while swirling a glass of fine single-malt whiskey.

But he had to settle for a Scrabble board, rather than a black and white board, and a plastic tumbler full of cheap lemonade stood in front of him.

Scrabble had become the old men's nightly sporting challenge.

Oodles did have a deck of cards and a crib board.

But trouble struck after three games of crib when they realised seven of the cards were missing.

Scrabble was the word game that made plebs feel like intellectuals, but James had to kill time somehow.

Tick, tock, tick, tock.

James scoured the board, looking for an opportunity. Finally, he built on Oodles's 'O' to make the word 'S O L E'.

Oodles looked at him like he had lost his mind. "Why would you waste an 'S' on such a tiny word?"

"Why don't you just do your job as scorer and write it down?"

James snarled. "There's no law that says you can't use your S at the start of words. Four points is four points."

The truth was he was trying to set himself up. He already had an 'M' 'I' 'S' and 'C' and if he had the chance he would add them to 'S O L E' next move. That would make the word 'S O L E C I S M', which would take him to a triple-word score.

He knew the others would dispute the validity of the word.

But what could they do? There was not a dictionary in the house. They would just have to accept his word meant 'incorrectness of speech' and accept the superiority of his linguistic skills.

Wish-Wash looked up from his palette and gave a big, cheesy grin. Then he put down a single tile, with a dramatic flourish like he was laying the last brick of the Taj Mahal.

James sucked in a breath sharply. "That is not a proper word."

"Sure it is, isn't it Oodles? 'R S O L E'. Look it up in the dictionary, Jimbo. You'll probably get a mention in the explanation."

"You know we have not got a dictionary."

"I can't help that." Wish-Wash glanced at Oodles. "We'll have to vote on it, eh, cobber?"

Knocking on the front door interrupted them.

Oodles cocked his ear. "Who would that be at this time of the night?"

Katy had already been. She had left a lamb casserole at the front door, and rung the doorbell like she normally did.

Oodles had come to accept she'd deliver the evening meal every day.

But it had irked him for the first few days locked up together.

"It's not like I can't cook," he said. "Even Madge used to let me cook my signature dishes once or twice a week."

"Didn't all those dishes come out of a tin, cobber?" Wish-Wash said.

"So? Baked beans keep you regular."

"Maybe," Wish-Wash said. "But I don't think it's a good idea to subject us to them for a whole three months. Not when we've only got one dunny."

The knocking continued.

"You'd better answer it, Clarence," James said.

"Me? Why me?"

Knock-knock, knock-knock.

"It's your house."

"That doesn't mean anything." Oodles glanced at Wish-Wash. "Does it, old mate? I say we put this to a vote, too."

"Oh, this is ridiculous. Juvenile!" James stood up and looked around the room. "Where is my face mask?"

Knock-knock, knock-knock.

Wish-Wash pointed to the top of the china cabinet. "There. With mine and Oodles's."

James walked over to them and his voice became shrill. "They are all mixed up! How the dickens am I expected to know which one is mine?"

"Does it flamin' matter?" Wish-Wash said.

"Of course it matters! I have not got a clue who I will find when I open the door. I would feel a lot safer if I were wearing my own mask."

"Just take a guess at which mask is which," Wish-Wash said. "That's what I do and it hasn't killed me yet."

Knock-knock, knock-knock.

———

Taking the mask from the top of the pile, James strapped it on as he walked towards the front door.

When he opened up, he came face-to-face with a big-smiling man with a six-pack of cans in the crook of his left elbow and wearing a suit that was remarkably similar to the ones James had at home.

"Ta da. I'm out of isolation, cuz." Conn Northan turned sideways and poked out his right elbow. "Dis new style of handshake is going to take some getting used to, eh?"

"You?" James gave him a smouldering look and left the elbow unbumped. "Where is your mask?"

"I never knew'd I had to wear one now I'm out of self-isolation?"

"Why did you not answer the door every time my daughter came knocking?"

"I didn't open the door for anyone. Tanks, by the way, for giving me a place to self-isolate. I'm also much obliged you left so much food in the fridge and larder. Pity about the lack of beer. I don't normally drink Scottish malt, but beggars can't be choosers."

James squeezed his eyes shut.

He opened them when he felt something cold brushing against his hands.

"I've brought you some medicine," the Irishman said, pressing the six-pack forward. "I presume you like Guinness?"

James looked down disdainfully.

"I was going to get you a six-pack of toilet paper, but Rose's Super-market has sold out and I thought these would at least take your mind off any sticky crisis dat might befall you."

James stood there speechless.

"No need to tank me. I was tinking. If you gave me the passcode for dat smart phone you left in the kitchen, I'd be able to call every day to check on you."

SIX
A ROOM OF HIS OWN
THREE WEEKS IN

AFTER THREE WEEKS, Oodles finally relented on the third bedroom.

He agreed to clean out the spare room so James could be by himself.

It was only a tiny space and the window did not even have blinds or curtains, but at least it gave James a retreat.

The room was full of junk, and it smelled musty, which was a contrast to the rest of the house where dust entered at its own risk of Oodles's feather duster.

You never knew the extent of someone's foibles until you had to live with them. The first time James had sorted his washing after clearing the clothesline, Oodles had looked at him in bemusement. "Aren't you going to iron those underpants, old son?"

Oodles even ironed towels and tea towels, which were folded and packed away in their respective drawers according to colour from dark to light.

Heaven forbid if you accidentally put a knife in the slot where the forks were supposed to go. Oodles rarely went off but you could see his distress, and he simply had to repair the damage before he could concentrate on anything else.

The spare room revealed a secret when the old men were swapping furniture around.

In the corner was a TV that Oodles had not even known about.

It came with a VHS player on top.

"I'll be buggered," Oodles said. "That would explain why it sometimes sounded like Madge was jumping around in there."

"I get worked up like when I watch some westerns," Wish-Wash said. "Was that her caper, too?"

"I doubt it," Oodles replied. "It's more likely she was watching lawn bowls or gardening."

"And she was jumping around?" Wish-Wash said. "Seriously?"

The writing on the front indicated it was a colour TV, but that was a moot point because they soon discovered it would not work without being attached to an aerial.

They had spent half an hour pulling out furniture in the living room looking for somewhere to plug in the coaxial cable before Oodles remembered he had never actually had an aerial installed on the roof.

Wish-Wash suggested they enlist young Tim Noah to help. James thought he vaguely recognised the name but when Oodles explained the kid was working as an intern at the Tasmanian Tiger Museum and actually came from the United States he realised he could not possibly know him.

"Is he any good?" James asked.

Oodles shook his head. "We don't call him Awesome Sauce for nothing. Though you might call that irony."

Wish-Wash rang him, and handed the phone to James.

As Oodles had insinuated, the teenager did not lack confidence. He diagnosed the aged TV needed a set-top box to convert the signal from analogue to digital. He could do that but he would also have to install an aerial on the roof.

"You do know you cannot actually enter the house," James said.

"But I'll have to," the American twanged. "OTHERwise, all you'll be able to do is play videos on the VHS player."

"That's what we will have to do. Thank you anyway." James saw Wish-Wash's face crumple as he said it, then hung up.

The old men searched high and low for the videos.

Oodles said he had not seen them among the things they had carted out of the spare room.

Mind you, he probably had not given it his full attention. That was because he was the one with a spanner. It was a good thing someone knew how to dismantle and reassemble the single bed from the other room.

SEVEN
FRESH AIR
FOUR WEEKS IN

WISH-WASH SNAPPED the elastic loop from around his ears and tore off his mask. "It's not the same, is it?"

Oodles removed his mask, too. "What's not the same, old mate?"

James lowered his mask just enough so he could talk. "For goodness sake, what's the point of even wearing these damn things if we keep taking them off."

The three old men were sitting on the green bench in the garden. It had probably been designed for two adults and a child. James was squeezed between the other old men.

Even though it was uncomfortable, it was good to be outside.

Maddie had said it was OK for them to sit in the garden as long as they wore their masks and did not go past the front gate.

Wish-Wash waved the mask he had torn off. "No one can understand a word I'm saying with this flamin' thing on."

"Really?" James said. "You say that like it's a bad thing?"

"I'm getting cabin fever. When we used to sit on the park bench in the High Street, we could see exactly who was going where and when. But what can we see here?" Wish-Wash pointed to the green basin sitting on the green pedestal in the middle of the green lawn. "The comings and goings of Oodles's bird bath?"

"Strewth!" Oodles said. "What have you got against birds?"

"Nothing. But seen one bird, seen 'em all," Wish-Wash said.

Oodles rubbed the back of his neck. "That's not true though is it, old son. How many Green Swift Parrots have you seen today?"

"How the heck would I know? Birds all look the same to me."

"I'm pretty sure the Green Swift Parrot is green," Oodles said. "Seen any of them?"

Wish-Wash, dressed in his pink floral shirt and his orange and swirly green track-suit pants, puffed himself up to his full sitting height. "You know I flamin' haven't. Otherwise you would have seen it, too."

"Not necessarily," Oodles said. "I might have blinked. They don't call it a Swift parrot for nothing."

James shifted uncomfortably. This was yet another example of the sparkling wit and repartee he was now subjected to.

Oodles asked: "How are you sleeping in that new room, old mate?"

"Wonderful. You?"

Oodles shook his head. "I can't remember the last good night sleep I had. Goes with my age, I suppose. I'm surprised it hasn't caught up with you blokes yet. At least I'm still dreaming so I must be getting *some* shut-eye." A smile formed as he locked eyes with James. "Be buggered if that hasn't just broken a memory. I dreamed about you the other night."

"Me?" James said. "Are you sure it was me?"

"Yes. You were back in jail, but this time you had a ball and chain tethered to your ankle. Do you think it means something?"

"Only that you are losing your marbles!" James said.

Wish-Wash's voice came from the other side. "You look like you're sitting on a cactus, Jimbo!"

"I'm just trying to breathe. Is that all right?" James would have waved his hands for effect but one of them was trapped in the narrow crevice between him and Oodles, much closer to Oodles's left buttock than he had ever hoped to be located.

"You're not still angry about the Scrabble game last night?" Wish-Wash said.

"I'm only angry at myself for agreeing to play with a known cheat!" James spat.

"It was an honest mistake," Wish-Wash said. "You know my eyesight isn't so good close up."

James had known something was amiss when he studied the board looking for a word to build on late in the game, and realised six blanks had been laid down. How could that be? Scrabble only had two blank tiles that are unmarked and carry no point value but they can stand in to be any letter.

He had examined both Wish-Wash's and Oodles's faces for an explanation, and the big man had cracked first. He admitted he might have accidentally placed a couple of letters the wrong way around.

A couple! Seeing as James had one of the two blanks on his rack, it had to be at least five mistakes!

And it turned out to be even worse than that.

Oodles revealed he had the other blank.

When James turned the offending blanks over, they revealed an 'M', a 'B', 'an N" an 'F', a 'K', a 'C' and a 'U'.

Wish-Wash had argued this was proof of his honest mistakes. He said he could have made some perfectly good words with those letters, possibly on triple-word squares.

"I just don't know why you did not put on your reading glasses to play!" James snarled.

"I traded those stupid things in for a nice necktie."

"You what?" James's facial muscles exploded. "You needed those glasses a lot more than a tie. What are you going to do with it? Use it as a belt?"

"Thanks for the idea, Sherlock. You can't use a pair of specs to hold up your trousers, can you?"

"No, but they would help you to see the writing on the tiles."

James turned to Oodles. "Do you think someone can make an honest mistake six times?"

Oodles picked at the peeling green paint on the armrest like he was deep in thought. He noisily breathed in air through his nose and exhaled slowly. "What else are you going to do every night, old son? Scrabble kills about two hours of our time. If Wish-Wash says it was an honest mistake, he deserves the benefit of the doubt."

James's face dropped. "Really? I hope you two will be happy playing together. If you need me, I'll be in my room reading."

"Tonight?" Oodles said.

"Every damn night!"

"Reading?"

"That's what I said. If you're silly enough to play with a known cheat, be it on your own head."

Oodles leaned back and thought. "Speaking of reading, old son, you don't think it's odd Conn bought your e-reader but not your clothes?"

"The thought certainly has crossed my mind." James looked down at his knees, which reminded him he had been reduced to wearing Oodles's overalls, and he suspected Conn was indeed working his way through his wardrobe and wearing his suits. "But what can I do about it locked up here?"

The now nattily-dressed Irishman had not even brought the right e-reader.

James had given him precise instructions where to find his new model, but he had delivered his old one, which was not only loaded with books James had already read but had the battery life only slightly longer than a goldfish's memory.

But no way was he going to confess this to his housemates because he knew they would think it was actually funny.

James tried to wriggle into a more comfortable position. At least, the weak April sun was on his face, and the air was fresh for a change.

"Will you look at that?" Oodles's exclamation turned the others' heads. He was inspecting a shard of green paint that had come off in his fingers. He rubbed his fingers together and sighed heavily. "That time has come around again."

EIGHT
THE SECRET PYRAMID

THE BACK of his ute came into sight when Oodles rolled up his garage door.

Only when he switched on the fluorescent light did everything else become clear. One of the walls was full of tools, all hanging from corresponding black-painted shapes. The car had been polished until you could almost call it a mirror, and the concrete floor looked like you could eat off it. Then James saw the pyramid of paint cans in front of the car.

The old men flattened themselves to slide past the side of the car to get a better look. "There must be 100 tins here," Wish-Wash gasped.

"One hundred and seventeen," Oodles corrected him.

"How can you be so precise?"

"I used 15 the last time I painted the house," Oodles said. "Then I used one to paint the bench, the bird bath and anything else I could find."

Wish-Wash picked up the tin from the top of the pyramid and inspected it. "Why do you have so many gallon tins of paint?"

"3.78 litres each, actually," Oodles corrected him. "We had already gone to metric measurements when the Windy Mountain Council bought this lot in the early '90s."

"What did you just say?" James said.

Wish-Wash raised his voice. "Haven't you got your hearing aids in, Jimbo?"

James raised his hands and pointed to both his ears simultaneously. "Of course I have." He glared at Oodles. "But it could be my ears are deceiving me even with them in."

Oodles held his gaze. "I feel better finally getting this off my chest."

James squeezed his eyes shut. He had been mayor in 1991 when rumour had it the State Government was going to impose a 10 per cent sales tax on all tins of paint. So it seemed like a smart deal to write a council cheque for 300 tins and save money. Oodles was council works foreman, so he was tasked with finding storage for the stockpile and then dispensing it.

When the Mayor opened his eyes, Oodles was jutting out his jaw. "Do you know how far 300 tins of paint stretches, old cock? We painted the whole town green. Green buildings, green benches, green play equipment, even green rails around the football oval. The council was never going to get us any new colours until that lot was all used up."

James gasped. "I can't believe you stole it!"

"It's not like I backed a truck up to the shed. I only took one tin at a time home. It took me ages. Even then, I sat on my stash for years."

James kept glaring at him.

"Can you blame me? People would have been right on to me if my blue-and-white house became a green house a few weeks after my retirement. I had to keep schtum for a good 10 years after I got my gold watch."

"As I thought. Theft," James waggled a trembling finger. "Don't think you can drag me into your skulduggery."

"Drag you into it?" Oodles started counting his fingers. "One: I doubt the present council would give a fig about a few tins of paint going A.W.O.L. all those years ago. Two: With the charges over the pub burning down still hanging over your head, this pales into insignifi-cance. Three: You're already dressed for the task ahead. I knew there was a good reason to lend you those overalls."

James looked down. "These rags?" His finger trembled again. "Oh, no! As soon as my suit comes back from the cleaners, you can have this sack back."

"You're going to look bloody silly, old son, painting the house wearing a pin-stripe suit."

"Don't *old son* me," James spat. "I have no intention of aiding and abetting a criminal."

"Is that so?"

"As soon as this lockdown ends, I'll be going straight to the police station to report you."

Oodles grinned. "You won't have to. I think you'll find Stretch and his constables will be waiting outside with a set of handcuffs when the three months is over. Messerschmitt's not going down alone."

"You think the court will believe his grubby word over a distin-guished person like me who has an unblemished record."

Oodles smiled again. "Unblemished? You've never heard of corrup-tion? I wouldn't reckon I'm the only bloke in town who knows where you bought all this paint? Get a good price from your brother-in-law, did you? I'm sure you'll enjoy explaining to Stretch how you escaped paying sales tax!"

NINE
TIGER, TIGER

JAMES'S EYES were full of fear as he watched Oodles place the plank between the bottom rungs of the two ladders.

"I could break my neck if I fall off that narrow thing," James shrieked.

He could tell Oodles was considering his reply as he prised the lid off a tin of green paint with a paint-encrusted stick. He balanced the tin on top of the plank, and began stirring with the same stick. "It's not nearly as high as it will be, but if working off the ground worries you, old mate, you can stay on terra firma and keep painting the low bits."

"Does that mean you will be up there risking life and limb?"

"I've never fallen of a ladder yet."

"You never had to walk along a plank using a walking stick before!"

"I don't use it on the ground, why would I need it now?"

"Oh, maybe because Dr Jenkins *said* you ought to!"

"And you follow doctor's orders to the letter, too?"

"I most certainly do." James turned his head to Wish-Wash. "Where will Bert be working, anyway? Not down with me, I hope?"

"What's wrong with that?" Wish-Wash said.

James put his hands on his hips. "I'm getting a little sick and tired of your childish behaviour, Bert. I suppose you think painting noughts and crosses on my back is funny?"

"Is that what you think I've been doing?" Wish-Wash smirked. "You just can't take a joke!"

"You're not the one with a wet back," James said. "It's not as if these overalls even belong to me."

Wish-Wash glanced at Oodles. "You don't mind, do you cobber?"

Oodles rubbed the back of his neck and exhaled. "No, but James will have to stay outside till he dries. I only washed that floor this morning and I don't want any drips of paint messing it up again."

Wish-Wash started chortling again. "I've got lots of spare clothes in my wardrobe, which I'd be happy to let you hire, Jimbo."

"Hire?" James looked at him quizzically.

"I do need to recoup my dry-cleaning costs."

"Oh, right! Some of those old clothes might fall apart if someone ever tried to clean them!"

"That's nice, that is. It's no skin off my nose if you want to stay out here all night drying, Jimbo." Wish-Wash pointed to the edge of the backyard where the lawn merged into bushland that extended up the hill. "You just better hope Moose Routley isn't out hunting tonight and mistakes you for a Tasmanian Tiger."

"He knows perfectly well what I look like."

Wish-Wash looked at Oodles and started laughing like a donkey again. "But he's never seen you with stripes on your back before."

James frowned. "Stripes?" As soon as he said it, it dawned on him what the artwork on the back of his overalls really was. He should have known.

James had no idea how many stripes Tasmanian Tigers were supposed to have but he guessed he had now been given a full quota.

"Why do you not grow up, Bert," he snarled. "You and Clarence are the only people on earth who believe the Tasmanian Tiger is not extinct."

"How come people are always reporting sightings?"

"All the plebs are looking for their 10 minutes of fame, I suppose."

————

The front doorbell rang and Wish-Wash rubbed his stomach.

Painting had finished for the day and they had packed away the equipment and washed up.

"That'll be Katy with our dinner," Wish-Wash said.

"No kidding." James was draped in a blanket on the other end of the couch. He had shed his wet overalls at the back door, but the increasing cold had forced him to cover up his Y-fronts and singlet. "Who else would it be? Jehovah's Witnesses?"

"I doubt it," Wish-Wash said. "With the lockdown, they must be all working from home."

"Oh, very droll, Bert. Do not give up your day job." James looked over at Oodles in the armchair on the other side of the room. "What is it you two do, anyway, now you've been shamed out of the Tasmanian Tiger Museum?"

"Never you mind," Wish-Wash said. "You just fetch the lasagne."

James looked at him sharply. "How do you know it's lasagne?"

"Katy told me," Wish-Wash said. "She was over at the museum when Moose called me this morning asking for some pointers."

"Why would a moron like him call an imbecile like you for advice?"

"That's for me to know and for you to find out."

James raised his eyebrows. "What are you two up to?" he said slowly.

Wish-Wash folded his arms. "What makes you think we're up to anything? Just fetch our lasagne before it goes cold."

James tugged at the blanket that was wrapped around him. "What if this thing slips?"

"Who's going to see you?" Wish-Wash said. "You know Katy leaves the food on the mat, then goes."

James cocked his ear towards the window. "How come we never heard her car leave?"

"Maybe you forgot to turn your hearing aids on again?"

"You are like a broken record, Bert."

Wish-Wash shrugged. "Perhaps she walked today?"

"Carrying a full tray all the way up the hill? You are kidding me!" James stood up, turned around and lent over the couch so he could snap open a slat of the off-white, aluminium Venetian blinds. Why they called them Venetian blinds was beyond him? When he thought of Venice, he thought of gondoliers and Gothic architecture with elegant arches. The idea for blinds with horizontal slats might indeed have come from somewhere near the Grand Canal but this particular example had probably gone out of fashion in the Windy Mountain cul-du-sac around 1965.

"Hey," Oodles protested. "I spent ages cleaning those blinds. I don't want your greasy fingerprints all over them, old cock."

"Oh, relax." James reached back and waved a hand. Katy was leaning on the side of her ridiculous little car parked under a street-light with her mobile phone to her ear. "She's on the blower. Who do you think she is talking to?"

"How would I know?" Wish-Wash said. "Sergeant Stretch?"

James turned his head. "Why would she be talking to the police?"

Wish-Wash maintained his poker face. "He's going to want to know the address to send his men with the handcuffs to."

James huffed and turned back to the gap in the blinds he was holding apart. "My godfather, she has turned sideways. No one told me she was pregnant!"

"I thought everyone knew that," Wish-Wash said. "She's got to be three or four months gone now."

James kept peering. "No one told *me*!"

Wish-Wash chortled. "I guess you're not in the inner circle. She broke the news to us when we came back from Ireland."

James released the blind with a crack, and turned around again. "I knew nothing good would come of that union with that scruffy husband of hers. The Irish are reclaiming Windy Mountain one person at a time."

Wish-Wash blew out his cheeks. "Bloody heck, Katy is a fourth-generation Windonian!"

"We all know where the McDonnells came from. From across the ocean on a convict fleet!" James said.

"Haven't you got a short memory, Jimbo! Your ancestors probably shared a cabin with them."

"Whatever you say, Bert. What we know for *a certainty* is her husband is straight off the boat from Dublin."

"I think you'll find Joffa has spent more of his life in Australia than Ireland," Wish-Wash said.

"I am not sure being in an Australian jail counts as residency," James said. "They will probably make Conn the godfather. That is how these diasporas start."

Wish-Wash pointed to the door. "Will you just get the tucker. I'm starving. I can't help it if you didn't work up an appetite today. "

"I did my fair share." James looked pleadingly at Oodles. "Didn't I, Clarence?"

Oodles shook his head. "Beats me how you can get to 82 and have never used a paintbrush before. But there you have it! We've all got to start somewhere."

James went out into the corridor and turned on the external light switch by the front door. When he opened up and looked down, a large baking dish covered in tin foil sat on the mat. The steam wafting up indeed did smell like lasagne.

Katy turned and waved He smiled awkwardly, holding on tight to his blanket, and watched her climb into the car and close the door.

Wish-Wash shouted from inside. "What are you doing out there?"

"What do you think I'm doing?" James stooped to pick up the tray. He heard Katy's car drive off. When he looked up, her tail lights were fading away.

He brought the tray inside and laid it on the polished yellow and white-flecked laminate tabletop Oodles had cleared.

———

Oodles took three willow-pattern plates from the cupboard and cut three slabs of lasagna that he transferred with a metal spatula.

Wish-Wash launched straight into Grace. By the time he had finished saying "ten four six eight, bog in, don't wait," he was already spraying bits of lasagne over the table.

James flicked away a bit of food that had lodged in his blanket. "Really, Bert, that's a most disgusting habit."

Wish-Wash swallowed. "Fussy, fussy, fussy." He pointed his knife towards James. "You'll have me eating dinner in one of them face-masks next."

———

When Oodles cleared the used plates away, out came the Scrabble board.

"How many times do I have to tell you, I'm out!" James said.

Wish-Wash locked eyes with him. "How else will we decide who does the dishes?"

"Since you have got out of it every night by cheating, I think it is well past your time." James turned to Oodles. "But if you two still want to settle it by playing Scrabble, be my guest. I have got a new book to catch up on."

———

James could not remember the last time he had laid on a bed in silence and read uninterrupted for a decent amount of time.

It certainly had never happened when he was sharing the bedroom next door.

He was always distracted by the peripheral sight of Wish-Wash holding his encyclopaedias three inches away from his eyes.

When the big oaf came to an entry he liked he insisted on reading it aloud. You would think he was delivering Hamlet's soliloquy. His inflections breathed unexpected life into the most turgid entries. James supposed it could have been worse. If it had been sci-fi, Wish-Wash would probably have attempted all the voices, even the robots.

James pressed on. He was up to page 57 off *Far From the Madding Crowd*, by Thomas Hardy, which Maddie had left for him, probably trying to make up for her earlier ridiculous gift.

He had given her both barrels over the phone.

"Do you think I'm a child?" he had berated her. "Have you ever seen me doing a jigsaw?"

"Oh, Daddy! It's not like it's a 50-piece SpongeBob Squarepants jigsaw. I thought you'd enjoy a nice cultural Parisian scene. It's a thousand-piece puzzle designed just for adults."

"For goodness sake, the cover on the box depicts cyclists riding past the Arc de Triomphe. What has that got to do with French culture?"

"Don't be silly, Daddy. The jigsaw puzzle might be just the thing to amuse you on a rainy day."

"It's never going to happen. You hear me?"

The next day he had found the paperback on the mat.

The note with it said it was an early birthday present, but you could not fool him. Maddie's mother had been the same. She always made him a cooked breakfast the morning after an argument.

The paperback made a nice change from reading on his sub-standard e-reader.

When James finally put it down and glanced at his Rolex, it was 8.15pm.

He got up and walked to the window to open it, and realised someone had either left the back light on or a cat had triggered the sensor.

He stood there squinting across the lawn, but saw no sign of a cat.

What he did see startled him.

Just where the garden melted into bushland stood an animal he had only ever seen in books or on flickering black and white film.

His chest tightened. Was his angina returning?

He blinked slowly, hoping it was just a trick of the light.

When he opened his eyes, a Tasmanian Tiger was still there looking back at him. What's more, it was wearing a surgical mask!

TEN
THE WALLS HAVE EARS

HIS QUIVERING voice was giving him away over the phone.

"Are you all right, Daddy? You sound like you've just seen a ghost!"

Maddie was closer to the truth than she knew. But whatever James had seen outside his bedroom window last night, it had stripes, not a sheet over its head.

What was he supposed to say? *"I think I have seen a Tasmanian Tiger."*

No way was he going to confess to that, especially when he knew who was probably listening.

Wish-Wash was supposed to be out the front helping Oodles with the painting work. But when James had excused himself at 2.30pm to go take his daily call with his daughter, Bert had blurted that he also needed to go inside "to siphon the python!"

James now held the receiver close to one ear and listened to the noises of the house with the other ear. Thanks to his hearing aids, the toilet flushing had been loud and clear. But it was what he had not heard that worried him. Wish-Wash had never been able to leave the house without slamming the door, so it was very likely he was either lurking around a corner or using a glass against a wall to earwig from an adjoining room.

Bert had given him the Spanish Inquisition at breakfast.

The questions had come at greater rapidity than the coco-pops flying out of Bert's mouth.

"Are you enjoying sleeping in your own room, Jimbo?"

What was he up to? And was Oodles in on it? He seemed to be lost in eating his toast and didn't even respond to James's puzzled look.

"No one is keeping me awake snoring, if that is what you mean, and I find it pleasant sleeping with the window open for a change."

"Wasn't it a bit nippy last night?"

"I was actually toasty warm with the thick quilt Clarence found."

"Goodo." Wish-Wash looked him in the eyes across the table. "But when you were opening the window, did you happen to see anything interesting outside?"

This was when James knew for sure some kind of tomfoolery was going on.

But he was not going to give Wish-Wash the satisfaction he sought!

James swallowed for dramatic effect. "As a matter of fact, I noticed the outside light was on. Is that what you mean?"

Wish-Wash smiled. "Anything else?"

James scratched his head in mock thought. "Yes, now you mention it, there was. You had left a pair of orange-and-swirly-green tracksuit pants hanging upside down on the clothes line."

Wish-Wash picked up his bowl and lifted it to his lips. After a long slurp, he asked James if he had seen anything else.

James lowered his voice to a whisper. "How did you know, Bert?"

Wish-Wash beamed at him.

James flashed a fuller set of teeth. "How did that Hawaiian shirt get on the washing line, too? I can't remember anyone wearing it for ages."

Maddie's words propelled James back to the phone call.

"I'm going to leave you something on the front mat tomorrow, Daddy. It should be there by the time you wake up."

"Another early birthday present?" James gasped. "I have not finished the last book."

"But this one isn't a book. And it's for all of you. I'm worried you and your friends aren't getting enough exercise."

"Friends? You jest!" he blurted, then he stopped himself, knowing the walls probably did have ears. "You know they are making me paint this house, which means I do vigorous exercise every day."

"Hmm," came the doubtful voice down the line. "I'm not sure where painting sits on the Heart Foundation's recommended exercise list."

"Really, Maddie! I would not have made it to 82 if I had not looked after myself. Remember the long walks I used to take Howard on?"

"But the family dog has passed on, Daddy, and you've never been in self-isolation for three months before."

"Do you have to remind me how long my period of incarceration is. It reminds me of being with your mother."

"Daddy!"

"Well!" His voice dropped. "Heard from her? I bet she and her new husband are not doing this tough like me. Prue's probably sitting by the pool in the Maldives maintaining social distance from the waiter by having her own bottle of gin."

"Daddy!"

"Well!"

"No, I haven't heard from her," Maddie said. "I doubt she's moved from their Point Piper apartment though. And another thing. He's hardly her *new* husband. They have to have been married for more than 30 years."

James blew out his cheeks. "If you say so." His tone changed. "You know, we really do not need some kind of fitness apparatus. We spent nearly two hours doing a treasure hunt this morning?"

"A treasure hunt?"

"That's what Bert wanted to call it, anyway. He is convinced Madge hid a cache of videotapes somewhere."

"Madge?"

"Oodles's wife. You remember her? Died in that fire?"

"Of course. Poor Oodles! How can you ever get over something like that?"

James screeched. "I lost my wife, too, and you do not hear me complaining!"

"That's different."

"How is it different? Sometimes I lie awake at night wishing Prue had been consumed by fire, too, rather than following the Pied Piper from Point Piper."

"Daddy!"

"Don't *Daddy* me. This is what close proximity to high-smelling paint does to you. It gives you black thoughts."

"All the more reason for you to do more to get your heart and lungs working harder. What I'm leaving for you will help with that."

"Goodness, Maddie, if I worked any harder I would probably spontaneously combust."

Maddie sighed. She probably had enough time to count to 10 during the long pause.

"What kind of videos are you looking for?" she asked.

"Old VHS tapes."

"But what are they about?"

"I simply do not have a clue. All I know is it is hard work dragging chairs around the house so you can get up and look on the tops of wardrobes."

"Are you eating well, Daddy?"

"You've got to be joking. You know what we had to eat last night? Lasagne! Howard used to eat better than I do now."

"All the more reason you need to up your exercise to burn the carbs, Daddy. Don't forget to check the front mat in the morning."

James heard the front door slam.

ELEVEN
THE EXERCISE BIKE

THE FUMES HIT James as soon as he went down the three front steps outside.

Oodles lowered his mask. "He returns!"

James waved a hand in front of his face to chase the fumes away. "Is it not about time to wind up, anyway? The light is already fading, and it really stinks out here."

"And who's fault is that?" Oodles glared at him.

James waggled a finger. "Oh no, you are not pinning that one on me."

"If you had bought water-based paint instead of spirit-based paint we wouldn't need to soak our rollers and brushes in smelly mineral turpentine."

"I got the best deal for the council!"

"And for your brother-in-law."

"Not this again? If it's any consolation, I do not speak to him any more, not since Prue, you know . . ."

"Buggered off and left you," came the voice behind him.

James looked around. Wish-Wash was squatting at an old blue ice-cream container, washing his brush in turps. He was wearing a smock

Henri Matisse might have worn, with dabs of yellow, red and blue on white cotton. It was remarkable what they sold at the Slutz Plains Op-Shop.

"Tactful as always, Bert!" James said. "Sniffing that turps cannot be good for the few brain cells you have got left."

Wish-Wash stood up flicking his paintbrush bristles, sending a shower of green spray towards the ground. "Don't worry about me, Jimbo. I'm not the one who hallucinated seeing a Tasmanian Tiger wearing a mask outside your bedroom window."

James opened his mouth but stopped himself. Now he knew for sure Wish-Wash was somehow behind all that, but he really wasn't going to give him the satisfaction. "I told you this morning: the only thing I saw was your clothing drying on the Hill's hoist. You're still making up stories, I see."

Wish-Wash stepped closer so his chin aligned with James's forehead. "What's that supposed to mean?"

James looked sideways at Oodles. "You're a witness to this. Bert is trying to intimidate me. Once the school bully, always the school bully."

"Knock it off, you blokes," Oodles said. "You're as bad as each other."

Wish-Wash stepped back.

Oodles dropped his voice. "Wish-Wash tells me your daughter is getting us an exercise bike, old son."

James pulled a face. "He said what?"

"I heard her say it," Wish-Wash protested.

"Heard it? How?" James asked.

"That's for me to know and for you to find out," Wish-Wash said.

"You'll have to find room for it in your room," Oodles said. "I can't think of anywhere else it can go. We'd need to give this house a dozen more coats of paint to clear enough space in the garage for something as big as that."

James stared at him. "As usual, Bert has added one and one together and got three."

Wish-Wash's eyes widened. "I know what I heard."

James shot back with a raised voice: "If you had been minding your own beeswax, you would not have heard anything to misinterpret. You only came inside on the pretext of going to the toilet."

"I had to wash my hands, which takes time," Wish-Wash said. "You ask Katy? She says good hand-washing hygiene is really important right now."

James held up all 10 of his fingers and thumbs, closed his fists and opened them again. "Twenty seconds is all you need. Twenty! You were in the house much longer than that."

"If you must know," Wish-Wash said. "I was waiting to use the phone. It's not your personal flamin' hotline. We know all about the direct line you used to have to Birty's house, don't we Oodles?"

"For goodness sake, I was the Mayor in those days. It was important I had a good means of communication with the local chief of police."

"I feel the same about who I wanted to speak to," Wish-Wash said.

"Who exactly?" James asked.

"That's for me to know and you to find out."

James bowed his head and pinched the bridge of his nose. "You really are like a broken record, Bert. As if I care?"

Wish-Wash stepped closer again, close enough for James to feel his breath on his face. "You hate my guts, don't you."

Oodles pushed them apart. "Knock it off, I said. Why don't you tell James the good news, Wish-Wash?"

Wish-Wash stuck out his bottom lip. "Why should I?"

"Because I think he'd be impressed."

James frowned. "What good news?"

"He found one of the videotapes," Oodles said.

James's eyes widened. "I thought we had looked everywhere. Inside every cupboard, the tops of every cupboard . . ."

"We never thought to look under my bed," Wish-Wash said.

James looked hard at him. "Under your bed?"

"I had to fill in my time somehow when you were hogging the phone, didn't I?"

"So you went looking under your bed?"

"Are you wearing your hearing aids, Jimbo?" Wish-Wash turned to Oodles. "You heard me say that, didn't you, cobber?"

"Under your bed!" James gasped. "The same bed that's against the wall that has the phone on the other side. What? Were you looking for your reading glasses you don't have any more!"

"How many times do I need to tell you, I don't need glasses. I can see just fine." Wish-Wash started heading for the front stairs. "If you don't mind, I've still got to make that phone call."

TWELVE
THE MYSTERY TAPE

WISH-WASH RUBBED HIS HANDS TOGETHER. "Right. Let's see what we've got then!"

They had finished their Sunday night beef roast with baked potatoes and Yorkshire pudding.

James stood up. "I think I will leave you chaps to it. I am halfway through a rather good book."

"Please yourself, Jimbo." Wish-Wash did another drum solo with his fingers on the videotape that laid flat on the yellow table. "But if you go you'll never find out what's on here?"

James put his hands on his hips. "I'm sure you will be dying to tell me in the morning, Bert?"

Wish-Wash shook his head. "Nope." He looked at Oodles across the table. "Isn't that right, cobber? He'll never know what he's missed out on, will be?" He looked back to James. "Be there or be square."

James heaved a sigh. "I will stay for the start then, and see." He walked over to his end of the sofa.

———

The videotape had no cover and no label, not even in Madge's handwriting.

Oodles guessed it was probably an episode of *Jack High* Madge had recorded from ABC-TV.

Wish-Wash wasn't convinced though. Why would Oodles have heard her jumping around to that? He couldn't believe lawn bowls would have brought out such high emotions.

Oodles got up from the table and started stacking up the dirty plates and cutlery.

Wish-Wash eyed him in disbelief. "Can't the washing up wait for once?"

"I won't be able to relax if I haven't done them, cobber." Oodles picked them up and disappeared into the kitchen, leaving James and Wish-Wash looking at each other.

"Are you not going to help him for once?" James asked.

Wish-Wash waved the video tape. "Don't you think I have enough to do? Someone's got to take charge of operating the flamin' VHR machine."

The sound of running taps came from the kitchen. "I'll be out in a jiffy," Oodles shouted. "These few dishes won't take me long."

When he emerged, he was wearing a striped red apron, and walked over to his armchair.

Wish-Wash was poised ready over at the VCR. He slid the mystery video into the slot and his hand hovered over the play button. He turned his head. "Ready? No one needs to go to the dunny?"

"Just get on with it, Bert." James said.

"Wait!" Wish-Wash said. "Shouldn't we have popcorn?"

"Will you get on with it, Bert," James said again.

"What about the lights? I'm not starting this until one of you blokes turn out the lights."

"For goodness sake." James got up and flicked the switch.

The video started.

It was a pirate tape of *Jane Fonda: Workout*, released in 1982.

Fonda appeared with big hair, a striped pink leotard, and with a group of men and women behind her copying her every movement.

"I remember this," Wish-Wash sank back into the other end of the sofa. "That Janey Fonda is a bit of all right." He tilted his head to the left. "How does she make her legs swivel like that?"

"Oh, for goodness sake!" James said. "She's got to be nearly as old as you are now, Bert."

Wish-Wash's face glowed from the light from the screen. "I suppose you're right. You reckon she can still make her legs swivel these days?"

James sighed heavily as he stood up to leave. "I really have better things to do. She looks more like the fourth member of The Bee Gees to me. All that hair and shrill."

Wish-Wash looked hurt. "You know it's a sign of bad character to quit on a video before it ends?"

"Really, Bert? I've only ever heard that wisdom applied to books," James said. "Which reminds me, if you'll excuse me, I really want to find out how *Far From the Madding Crowd* ends."

THIRTEEN
FITNESS HELPERS

"WE WATCHED IT TWICE, didn't we Oodles?" Wish-Wash said.

They were sitting at the table eating breakfast. The old brown radio in the kitchen played a mournful country song in the background.

Surely, Wish-Wash would come to the bottom of that box of coco-pops soon? Mind you, if he had picked up the ones he sprayed on the floor and recycled them he could probably make them last as long as the blue singlet he slept in and wore to breakfast each morning.

"You sure missed a good show last night, Jimbo," Wish-Wash said.

"I saw enough, thank you." James continued buttering his toast.

Wish-Wash winked across at Oodles. "But you missed the twist ending, didn't he cobber?"

"Lots of twists and turns, actually," Oodles agreed.

Wish-Wash beamed. "She has a lovely ending, that girl."

James clenched his eyes shut. "I'm trying to eat my breakfast. Can you not act your age? Anyone would think you are related to that sleaze-bag Billy Gumboots." He opened his eyes. "Oh, I forgot. He was your . . . " he made quotations in the air with his fingers ". . . love-child."

"You're just jealous," Wish-Wash said.

"Jealous that you once had a quickie with the town bike?"

"I'll have you know Marta Kretocek was the light of my life."

"What light was there behind the Slutz Plains dance hall, pray tell? The way I heard it, it was a shot in the dark."

"Will you knock it off, old son!" Oodles said. "It was such a long time ago, and we have no real evidence Billy was even Wish-Wash's son."

"Really?" James held Oodles's gaze. "So you're saying their similar appearances and mannerisms might have just been a co-incidence."

Wish-Wash covered his ears. "Sticks and stones might break my bones, but names will never hurt me."

"Oh, do you have to be so childish, Bert," James muttered. "Even your broken noses sloped the same way."

Wish-Wash dropped his hands to the table. "You're the one being childish, Jimbo. You're the one now with the bike."

"For goodness sake, what are you talking about, Bert?"

"You heard me, you deaf git. That exercise bike Maddie is leaving is all yours. Oodles and I have decided to do our workouts along with Janey's video from now on. That's all the exercise we'll need."

"You are joking? That video was designed with women in mind."

"How do you explain there are two young blokes exercising in the background them." Wish-Wash poked his own chest. "The one who looks like me isn't even wearing a flamin' shirt."

James pinched the bridge of his nose. "I hope you're not planning to take your shirt off, Bert."

"What if I am? Anyway, you won't know. You'll be too busy with your town bike in your room."

James rolled his eyes. "How many times do I have to say it. There is no exercise bike. Which reminds me . . ."

He got up and went to the front door.

Down on the mat was a folded note and three plastic wrist-bands of differing colours.

———

James threw the bands on to the table. "Satisfied?"

Wish-Wash scratched his head. "I thought you said we were getting an exercise bike! How does Maddie expect these to help us exercise?"

James unfolded the note and perused it. "Apparently, they're all fitness trackers. Maddie says she's already set them up. The black one is mine, the blue one is Clarence's and the other one . . . "

Wish-Wash beamed. "How did she guess that green is my favourite colour?"

"Like father, like daughter, I suppose. She has a political eye," James said. "She's obviously seen you around often enough in your green trousers and green shirts to get a sense that you don't live in the same fashion world as other people."

Oodles picked up the blue band and examined it. "I'm still not getting this, old mate. How will this help with our exercise?"

James looked down at the note and moved his lips as he read on. When he got to the end, he looked up. "Maddie says they will measure the exercise we do. She says she's already linked us so we can make each other accountable."

"Linked us?" Oodles frowned. "What does that even mean?"

"I guess we'll find out as we go." James waved the note. "Apparently, they can record how many steps you do. I presume we'll be able to see how many steps each other has done."

"Steps? Pig's arse!" Wish-Wash screeched. "I told you, Jimbo. Me and Oodles plan to do the fitness workouts with Janey."

"Hmm." James said. "Looks like you're in luck. This note says you can measure other types of fitness sessions, too."

"How?"

"Hmm, she doesn't say." He stretched out the printed note and studied it again. But it didn't go into that detail. "I guess that's another thing we'll work out as we go. We can start right now by doing some laps outside of the house."

"I can't go outside dressed like this," Wish-Wash cried. "You two are dressed. You'll have to go alone."

FOURTEEN
RAISING HEARTBEATS

OODLES AND JAMES were puffing on their return from two brisk laps of the house.

When they walked into the lounge room they were surprised to find Wish-Wash wheezing, too.

"I got in a couple of minutes of Janey," he said, as he back-stepped from the VCR he had just switched off. "How did you blokes go?"

Oodles slumped into a chair and squinted at his watch. "It says we did 197 steps."

"Mine says 205." James had resumed his seat on the end of the couch. "Does that mean you've got a longer stride than me, Clarence?"

"Don't know." Oodles kept studying his watch. "Hey, this also measures our heartbeat."

"So it does," James said. "Yours is 76."

Oodles looked up startled. "How do you know that?"

"Maddie said we were linked! I guess that's what she meant about being accountable to each other. We cannot only see each other's steps, we can read everyone's heartbeat, too."

"So we can!" Oodles kept looking at his watch. "Yours is only 68, Jimbo. Very impressive, old mate."

They both seemed to notice Wish-Wash's heart-rate at the same time, and looked over at him.

"142!" James blurted.

———

"It was the exertion of getting up walking across the room to turn off the VCR that did it," Wish-Wash argued as he painted.

"Pull the other one." James was painting alongside him. "We both know what put your heart-rate up. Jane Fonda!"

He was interrupted by his fitness tracker vibrating. Wish-Wash's must have gone off, too, because he looked down at his wrist. Oodles was working on a plank high up but he seemed to come to a halt, too.

"What's going on?" he shouted down.

James studied his watch face. "Looks like the fitness trackers want us to do 250 more steps."

"What, now?" Oodles said.

James shrugged. "Do you want to risk being up there if the wristband gets angry? That gentle vibration might be just a warning. The next warning might be 7000 volts."

Oodles climbed down the ladder nearest to him, and the old blokes completed three laps around the house. Wish-Wash complained all the way. He said he was only doing it because he didn't want to risk being electrocuted.

If that had been the end of it, they might have quickly forgotten.

But the fitness tracker buzzed again the next hour, and every hour subsequent, demanding 250 more steps each time. It was like being in a boot camp.

———

Oodles collected the empty plates again. They had devoured the Shepherd's Pie Katy had left on the doorstep.

You couldn't get nearer to peasant food than Shepherd's Pie but what choice did James have? He had worked up an appetite painting and walking 1487 steps around the house.

Wish-Wash stood up. "If you two blokes don't mind, I'm going for an early night."

"What? No Scrabble, old mate?" Oodles asked.

"Not tonight. I'll let you two fight over who does the dishes."

They watched him disappear out the door, and his footsteps faded as he went down the hall.

When they heard his bedroom door slam shut, James and Oodles looked at each other.

"What's that about?" James asked.

"I guess he's even more tuckered out than us," Oodles said.

———

They were getting to the end of their Scrabble game when they heard the commotion.

The noise came from the direction of Wish-Wash's bedroom. It sounded like the kind of grunt you hear from weightlifters, and it was followed by a screeching sound.

Oodles was the first to process it. "Wish-Wash must have got his second wind. That bedroom window has been stuck shut for years."

"He would not let me open that window," James gasped. "He said he doesn't like the cold."

"He must have changed his mind," Oodles said. "He's like that, our Wish-Wash."

James went back to concentrating on his letters. How had he fallen so far behind? There were only eight tiles left in the box and he was nearly 50 points behind. He needed to find a spectacular word to leap ahead to an unlikely victory.

He scratched his head. "How does Bert get away with it? We have been locked up in this house for weeks and he has not had to do the dishes once. Not once."

He folded his arms in front of him and lowered his head trying to view his tiles from a different angle, hoping a word would suddenly present itself. As he did so, he caught sight of his fitness tracker and Wish-Wash's heart-rate.

"Look at this!" He stabbed at the watch face. "176 beats a minute!"

Oodles double-checked his tracking device. "Be buggered. It must be all that exertion from opening the window that's done that."

James looked across at him and held his gaze. "That's probably what he'd say if he knew what we knew."

Oodles chuckled. "You don't think that's the reason?"

"Think about it. That video has reawakened old passions in Bert."

The expression on Oodles's face morphed to shock as he pointed to the wall. "You don't think he's in there pulling the pud?"

"It's worse than that. Why wouldn't he tell us who he was calling yesterday? I'll tell you why. He was calling a woman. She came to his window so he could let her in surreptitiously."

"Wish-Wash doesn't know any women."

"Nonsense! What about that Marta trollop?"

Oodles clicked his tongue. "Strewth! He hasn't had anything to do with her for years. They even had a time-share arrangement for visiting Billy's grave."

James banged his fist on the table, making the Scrabble tiles on the board jump out of place. "Some other old tart then. He's probably paid her to dress in a striped pink leotard."

Oodles stared at the wall again. "You think?"

James banged the table again, making the game beyond repair this time. "It's not good enough. You and I haven't made the sacrifices we've made self-isolating just for that irresponsible clodhopper to put our lives in danger by letting someone introduce germs into our inner sanctum."

Oodles looked down at the messed-up board and frowned. "This isn't about you not wanting to do the dishes?"

James stood up, his fists still clenched. "Certainly not. This is a serious matter. He headed for the door. "I'm going in."

———

James knew there was no lock on the bedroom door. But he stopped at the threshold and put an ear to the oak panelling.

He could hear nothing.

Perhaps they had heard him storming down the hall and were holding their breaths?

They were probably hoping he would just go away.

He'd give them something to really take their breath away.

He turned the knob and pushed the door open violently.

———

Wish-Wash looked up from his book when James burst in. "Wrong room, remember?"

"You don't fool me, Bert. Where is she?"

Wish-Wash frowned. "Where's who?"

James opened the wardrobe. The only naked lady it revealed was on one of Wish-Wash's neckties, the one which incongruously also had palm trees and had hung on a rack at the Slutz Plains Op-Shop for years until he had swapped his reading glasses for it.

James parted the other clothes with a hand.

"Who do you hope to find in there?" Wish-Wash put his book down by his side.

James got down on all fours and looked under the bed. It hurt his joints, and revealed nothing but dustballs that were probably hiding from Oodles.

Wish-Wash grinned. "Janey isn't under there any more if that's who you're looking for."

When James levered himself to his feet, he noticed the curtains over the window were fluttering in the breeze. "I get it. She's escaped."

"Escaped?"

"You don't normally open the window."

"I think you'll find I do," Wish-Wash said. "Just not when I have to share a room with you. I wanted to give you extra incentive to leave ASAP."

James tapped his wrist-band. "How do you explain having a heart-beat of 176?"

Wish-Wash chortled. "Yes, I saw that. I'm at a very exciting section in this encyclopaedia." He tapped the book, which lay next to him on the bed. "It's about the history of jigsaws."

FIFTEEN
POSTMAN'S KNOCK
SIX WEEKS IN

THEY STOPPED PAINTING when they heard the stop-start noise of a motorbike coming up the hill.

Oodles looked down from his plank, which spanned the top rungs of the two rickety wooden ladders. "The postman is late this morning."

"How do you know it's the postie?" Wish-Wash asked. "It could be any flamin' biker."

The old blokes only had a sliver of a view to the road from that side of the house. A flash of fluro yellow jacket and red Australia Post motorbike went by.

"Christ Almighty! Did you see who that is?" Wish-Wash said.

"Not from here, no," Oodles said. "Who?"

"Gus Foot."

Oodles jumped down like an excited kid clambering out of a tree-house. "You sure? Why would he be delivering the mail?"

"Dunno." Wish-Wash stooped down to rest his brush in the blue ice-cream container full of turps. "If we're quick, though, we can catch him at the letterbox."

"Oh, for goodness sake," James grumbled as he followed them.

Both of them had figured out how to disable the 250-steps-an-hour demand from their fitness trackers, and they flatly refused to join James in his laps around the house.

But they obviously regarded Gus Foot as some kind of god worth meeting over the letterbox.

When Gus had first stopped in Windy Mountain with his motor-cycle gang in the early 1990s, he was actually called Foetus. But when his gang left town with his motorbike but without him, he had no choice but to move into a squat with Moose Routley. His life changed when he won a dairy cow. He sold the cow to raise enough money to buy a small stake in a dot.com company, which made him a wealthy man. Now he had set himself up as an investment advisor, adding respectability by dropping his awful nickname. As far as James knew, he had not made anyone else rich but he continued to rake in the dollars from gullible fools like Clarence and Bert.

Gus was sitting on his idling motorbike, with his helmet in one of his large hands and two letters in the other.

"Gus!" Wish-Wash shouted. "I knew I recognised the beard and ponytail! What are you doing here?"

Gus combed his greasy hair back with his free hand. "Times are tough in the finance business, Wishy."

"But why did you choose to become a postie of all people?" Oodles asked.

Gus shrugged. "They were looking for people who knew their way around town and had experience riding motorbikes."

He twisted the throttle of the out-of-gear red machine. His lips started to move before the roar had even subsided. " . . . not quite the beast I'm used to but I got a bit sick of sitting in my office waiting for clients. I still have bills to pay."

He eyed them up and down from the other side of the fence. "I expected that you blokes would be wearing masks?"

"Shhhh!" Oodles put a finger to his lips. "Don't tell Katy."

"Or Maddie," James added quickly.

"We've got masks," Oodles said. "But they're pains when we are trying to speak. We never go out the gate though."

Wish-Wash grinned. "I bet you were surprised to find us all here."

"Not at all," Gus said.

"You weren't?" Wish-Wash looked around at the others.

"Stretch told me you were all self-isolating together."

"Sergeant Stretch!" James gasped. "How did he even know we were all here?" He looked back at Wish-Wash who was smiling like the cat who had got the cream. "It was him you phoned?"

"Don't you think he has a right to know where all the villains are?" Wish-Wash said.

"How dare you?" James spat. "The real villain is already in jail pending trial. Messerschmitt burned down the pub, not me."

"That remains to be proven in court," Wish-Wash said.

Gus held out the letters. "Maybe these will throw some light on the situation."

Oodles stepped forward to take them but Gus pulled back his hand. "They're both for the Mayor."

"Me?" James looked from face to face. "Who else knows I' am here?"

Gus turned the envelopes over so he could inspect the backs. "Hmm, the Office of the Director of Public Prosecutions, apparently."

James gave Wish-Wash another death stare as he stepped nearer the fence to receive his letters.

"Any requests for your last meal?" Gus smiled as he strapped his helmet back on and revved the engine. "Gotta crack on with my round," he shouted. He wheeled around the cul-de-sac and disappeared back down the hill.

———

Wish-Wash looked over James's shoulder. "You'd think Gus would have hung around to find out what's in those letters. Isn't he curious?"

James spun around and clutched the letters to his chest. "Will you kindly go away, Bert. I am not opening them with you gawking."

"You don't think I have a vested interest." Wish-Wash stuck out his bottom lip. "The Applecart was my spiritual home."

"That's a laugh," James said. "By spiritual home, I presume you mean it was the place you drank too many glasses of top shelf."

Wish-Wash's bottom lip curled. "You know full well I only ever drank cider. But someone has to pay. We need to know what's in those letters."

"The big fella has a point, old son," Oodles said. "The way I see it you owe it to us to share. We're all sharing everything right now."

"Sharing? Sharing what?" James asked.

"This house for a start," Oodles said. "Our meals, the painting work, our Jane Fonda video, heck you're even wearing a pair of my overalls."

"What? I watched that video for all of three minutes." James pinched at the straps of the overalls as he glared at Wish-Wash. "I was not the one who spilled soup over my suit either. Can I help it if the dry-cleaners are finding it a hard stain to get out?"

"That's not my fault, old son. Will it kill you to tell us what's in those letters?"

———

James ripped open the first envelope. "I'm actually looking forward to my day in court just to see the looks on your faces when I clear my name."

He unfolded the letter inside.

His scowl became a smile as he read it.

He looked up. "What did I tell you? I'm innocent."

He waved the letter. "They say after *thorough* investigations, they have decided not to press any charges against me."

Wish-Wash's smile became a scowl. "Typical! You found a new smart-arse lawyer then? Or did you just get your daughter to bribe someone?"

"That is slander," James spat.

"It's only slander if someone else heard it, isn't it Oodles?" Wish-Wash said.

"But you did hear it, Clarence," James said.

"I'm not sure I heard it correctly, old son. What's in that other letter? Might it be some kind of backdown to say the first letter was sent out in error?"

"You never let up, do you? Pack mentality!" James ripped open the second envelope.

He unfolded the letter inside.

His scowl became a worse scowl.

"Well?" Oodles said.

"Oodles was right, wasn't he?" Wish-Wash said. "The first letter was sent in error."

James looked up. "Actually, you're wrong. It says nothing about that letter."

"How come you look even more miserable then than you usually do?" Wish-Wash said.

James scrunched up the letter into a ball. "You would not look too happy either if you had just been summonsed to give evidence against Messerschmitt. Now he is going to know for sure I ratted him out."

SIXTEEN
MESSERSCHMITT RETURNS

THE SOUND of heavy footsteps coming up the hill made them turn their heads.

James spluttered: "He *is* wearing another one of my suits."

James's Irish cousin Conn came to a halt in front of the gate and bent over gasping. When he rose, he was sweating profusely. "I don't know what to do."

James glared at him. "You can stop wearing my suits for a start, especially when you go for a jog."

Conn eyeballed him back. "You tink I like having to run up here? It's not like you left me with a car!"

James pinched at his overalls. "Look what I am reduced to wearing? Why I can I not have at least a couple of my suits?"

"You know dat's not my doing." Conn pointed towards the green house. "Maddie doesn't want anyting entering dat door dat might carry the virus inside."

"How come she never told me anything of the sort?" James said.

Conn shrugged.

"And why am I still waiting for you to bring me my mobile phone?"

"Ah, dat's why I ran up here to tell you." Conn looked down at his shoes.

"Tell me?"

"I tink your nephew must have taken it."

"My nephew?"

"Yes. Jonny Northan. He turned up on the doorstep looking for you."

James felt the blood draining from his face. "Messerschmitt?"

"Is dat his nickname?" Conn raised a hand high above his head. "Big fella. Muscles. Tattoos."

James threw his head into his hands. "I thought he was safely locked up in jail."

"No, he's out on bail."

James looked up and gasped. "He told you that?"

"I tink he was trying to scare me."

"Oh, yes, intimidation is his specialty."

"I've met fellas like dat before. The only way to handle dem is to humour dem and not ask too many questions." He changed his expression. "For instance, I didn't ask him what he's been accused of. Dat's none of my business . . . unless, of course, you want to tell me."

James swept his hair back with a hand. "Where do I start? Arson, hiding in the bush when he knew police had a warrant for his arrest, eating stolen goods, falsifying an archeological site, being an accessory to kidnap and attempted grievous bodily harm."

"Don't forget how he stole our bench," Wish-Wash said.

"And he dismantled the Colonel Richard Northan sculpture," Oodles said. "Don't forget that?"

"Oh, and the bastard tried to relocate the Tasmanian Tiger Museum," Wish-Wash said.

James turned and shouted. "You know all those things have been explained to the police's satisfaction. Misunderstandings, all of them."

"Misunderstandings? My arse!" Wish-Wash rolled his eyes. "Just because you were involved in them, you dismiss them as misunderstandings, when the truth is you had your lawyer make the charges go away!" He addressed Conn. "Did you know your cousin here is a killer?" He had flecks of white on his lips when he turned back to James. "Have you told Conn how you arranged for the local newspaper to report that Oodles and me were killed in that car accident?"

James smiled weakly at the Irishman. "You understand how mistakes are sometimes made, Conn?"

"Oh, dat I do. Dat I do. We all make mistakes. I'm just glad I found you in such a forgiving mood."

James looked at him with narrowed eyes. "For you letting Messerschmitt steal my mobile phone?"

"Yes, dat, too."

James frowned. "Too?"

"It wasn't my fault. When he knocked on the door with dat baseball bat in his hand, he wouldn't believe me when I said you weren't there. When I took him to your bedroom, I thought he'd notice you weren't there and just leave. But what happened is dat he sat down on your bed and said he'd wait. He's been in your bedroom for two nights now."

"In my bed?" James yelled.

"He tinks it's actually good timing because he has nowhere else to sleep now he's out on bail."

James buried his head in his hands again. "Oh, this is bad. This is really bad."

Conn broke into a smile. "You'll be pleased to know I've come up with a plan to get him out of the house."

James looked up, smiling. "You have? How?"

"I've given him dis address."

SEVENTEEN
FIREWOOD

Ring-ring, ring-ring …

"THAT'LL BE THE PHONE." Wish-Wash turned towards the front door.

"Oh, for goodness sake." James shouted after him as he trotted up the path. "If that's Taylor's Takeaway again, tell them I'm sick of their excuses."

Wish-Wash was reaching for the doorknob, but turned. "What if it's Messerschmitt?"

James searched Conn's face for evidence he had also passed on the phone number as well as the address but was met with a non-committal look. "Tell him I have gone. I have, er, left the country," he shouted.

The man in the Matisse smock disappeared through the door.

Ring-ring, ring-ring …

Oodles gripped James's shoulder. "Do you think he'll accept that explanation, old cock? Even Messerschmitt would know no one's allowed to leave the country at the moment."

"I think you over-estimate his intelligence, Clarence," James said.

"Oh, I forgot," Oodles said. "Thick-headiness runs in your family, doesn't it? I'm still trying to work out why your daughter would take your suit to Taylor's Takeaway for dry-cleaning."

"Really! Who's the thick one now? In times like these, businesses have to diversify. Gin manufacturers switch to making hand-sanitiser. Textile factories turn out surgical face-masks. Taylor's Takeaway is just filling a need in the absence of a proper dry-cleaning business in this town."

"Yeah, but it takes a leap of faith to go from greasy fish'n'chips to grease-free suits. Besides, you know who owns that place?"

"Indeed I do. I sold the business to Dave Jenkins in the first place."

"Did you? When?"

"About six years ago."

"Was your daughter the mayor then?"

"She was in her second term."

"And she was fine with the local undertaker becoming the new owner of the takeaway, was she?' Oodles continued to look him in the eye. "And now he's also doing dry-cleaning!"

All this time, Conn stood back, saying nothing, but his focus going from head to head like he was following a ping-pong ball.

The back-and-forwards came to an abrupt end when Wish-Wash's head reappeared at the door. "You have to come inside, boys. That wasn't Taylor's Takeaway or Messerschmitt on the phone. It was Moose. Him and Joffa will be here soon with the firewood."

"I'd better get going." Conn turned and started walking down the hill.

———

James snapped back one of the slats of the Venetian blinds so he could look out to the road.

"See any Tasmanian Tigers out there?" Wish-Wash said.

James turned around and glared at him. "There you go making up stories again. I never said any such thing."

"Give it time," Wish-Wash said. "What can you see then?"

James resumed peering out. "Whose ute is that they have brought the firewood in?"

Wish-Wash stepped behind him and twanged a higher slat so he could see out. "I knew you were deaf, but I didn't know you were blind. Didn't you know the Tasmanian Tiger Museum has an official vehicle now? Read the signage on the flamin' side."

It said *Windy Mountain Tasmanian Tiger Museum,* and it did indeed have a child-like illustration of something that might have been a Tasmanian Tiger.

"What did I tell you?" Wish-Wash said. "There *is* a Tasmanian Tiger out the window."

"Oh, very funny, Bert. That illustration could be anything. It could even be mistaken for one of your native cats."

Wish-Wash snapped his slat shut and stepped back. "That was an honest mistake, and you know it."

"I know nothing of the sort." James cracked his blind closed and turned around. "I also do not know how on earth suddenly they can afford to have their own ute. Was the museum not lurching towards bankruptcy when you two had to gift it to them?"

"Business has picked up," Oodles said.

James frowned. "I thought they were not even allowed to have customers right now. Surely the trickle of business has dried up completely?"

"They've switched to doing virtual tours," Oodles said. "They've tapped into the vast international market via the inter web. That Katy is one smart cookie. Moose and Joffa provide the brawn, but she definitely is the new brains behind the operation."

Wish-Wash puffed out his chest. "Yes, she's a worthy replacement for me."

The others looked at him.

"What?" Wish-Wash said. "You don't think I would have taken the same route given the same set of circumstances?"

"It's not a particularly new ute," Oodles said. "It looks shiny but that's only because Joffa did a spray-painting course while he was inside, and Awesome Sauce did the sign-writing."

"The American kid?" James frowned.

"Yeah, him." Oodles said. "You could be right about that dodgy illustration of a Tasmanian Tiger though. If Awesome Sauce did it, it might well be a native cat."

Oodles sighed noisily. "How long do you reckon Moose and Joffa will be here? Don't forget to remind me we haven't packed away our painting gear."

———

Moose and Joffa came and went several times over the afternoon.

It wasn't a quick process. Each new ute-load of firewood had to be unloaded, and taken to the back of the house where it was split and stacked.

They might have accomplished it sooner had they not stopped for afternoon tea and several smoko breaks.

James reluctantly agreed to participate in a few games of Scrabble just to kill some time.

The old men took to the blinds whenever the chainsaws and the squeaky wheels of the wheelbarrow went quiet.

"What are those cans they're taking out of that ice box? Beer?" James said.

"Never mind that," Oodles grumbled. "They've taken off their shirts. Goodness know what the neighbours will think?"

"They'll probably mistake them for us," Wish-Wash said. The others looked at him again.

They returned to the board.

EIGHTEEN
THE HITMAN COMETH

DARKNESS WAS FALLING by the time Moose and Joffa finally left, but there was enough light for the old blokes to inspect their handiwork out back.

The two giants had made quite an impressive woodpile, which would probably see them through their last six weeks in isolation.

The wood stove in Oodles kitchen burned 24/7, heating the hot water and keeping the living areas toasty warm provided the door to the hall was kept shut. That hallway, though, was a wind tunnel, and the bedrooms were often as cold as Siberia.

They had just returned to the living room when the sound of a car door closing intruded.

"Bewdy. That'll be Katy with our grub," Wish-Wash said excitedly, as the three of them made a beeline for the Venetian blinds.

They watched her from their vantage spots as she carried a basket containing their dinner up the path towards the front door.

Oodles had given up going into conniptions over the likelihood of the blinds being smudged with fingerprints, now he embraced it with gusto.

Katy definitely was getting fatter. "Good thing she had her brainwave about the virtual tours before the vagueness of pregnancy set in," James said.

Oodles scrunched his eyes shut. "You can't say that, old son!"

"I forget I've had a bit more experience with pregnant women than either of you. I didn't think Prue could get any more vague by the time she had Maddie. But I was wrong. By the time she had ran away with that merchant wanker, I think she had reached peak stupidity."

Wish-Wash rubbed his stomach. "What do you think is on the menu tonight?"

"Goodness knows," James said. "Looks to me like she was carrying a picnic basket." He snapped the slat closed and looked up to the ceiling. "Please don't let it be a Ploughman's Lunch. My indigestion couldn't come at pickled onions."

When Oodles laid the basket on the table and opened the lid, he stepped back to evade the burst of steam.

Oodles sniffed in the aroma. "Mmm, it's spaghetti."

James rolled his eyes. Not more peasant food!

"There's a hand-written note alongside it." Oodles started reading it and looked up. "Katy says she's testing out a new recipe."

"Great!" James said. "We are her laboratory rats!"

Oodles awkwardly read out its name. "Pasta ca' muddicca."

James pulled a face. "Which is?"

Oodles looked at the note again. "It's a Sicilian peasant dish." He looked up at the steaming bowl. "Bugger me! Who knew you could make pasta sauce from breadcrumbs and olive oil?"

————

It really was quite tasty. But James was never going to admit that.

It had enough garlic, red pepper flakes, parsley and anchovies, and cheese, lots of cheese, to make breadcrumbs quite flavoursome.

James pushed his empty plate away and stood up. "If you do not mind, I need to get some steps in."

Oodles gasped. "But it's dark outside."

"You're worried I'll get lost?" James feigned a laugh. "No need to worry. If I follow the walls of the house, I probably can do without a GPS."

"But you can't go," cried Wish-Wash. "We haven't played our final Scrabble game to decide who has to do the dishes."

"Goodness gracious me," James said. "Do we have to keep playing until you win? It's not our fault we've finally worked out how you've been cheating?"

They had been forced to play games of Scrabble all afternoon while Moose and Joffa were wheeling back and forwards with loads of firewood, and serenading them with their chainsaws. It was either that or accede to Wish-Wash's repeated suggestions they watch the Jane Fonda video instead.

"Seeing as you lost all of those games, Bert, I'd say it's about time you had your turn with the dishes," James said. "I've really got other things on my mind and the walk will help me to clear my mind."

"You're worried about Messerschmitt, eh?" Oodles said.

"I cannot for the life of me work out why they have even let a dangerous criminal like him out of jail," James said. "I have to work out how to get him out of my house. If I set my lawyers on him, will that prejudice his forthcoming trial?"

James headed for the door. "I will fetch my jumper from my bedroom, and I will switch on the front and back lights."

"Goodo," Oodles said. "Mind how you go."

———

The back of the house was lit up like an airport runway when James laced up his shoes and contemplated which way around the house he should go.

He decided to go clockwise for a change of scenery.

The problem with this was it was hard to see anything when he rounded the house and came to the dark side.

He stopped and squinted into the shadows.

This was where they had been painting today, and he knew two ladders were lurking somewhere in the murk.

He knew, too, there was also no actual path, just a trampled lawn between the side of the house and the bushes along the fence-line.

He sighed heavily and turned on the light of his fitness tracker.

He had only done 52 steps.

He'd never hear the end of it if he went back inside. He knew what Wish-Wash was like. He'd be forever reminding him he was afraid of the dark.

No, he had to go on.

He stretched out his arms and started taking tentative steps forward. At least it was uphill, which meant speed and momentum weren't problems. But he could not see a thing.

A twig snapped, and he stopped.

When he heard nothing, he decided it must have been a possum scaling a tree. A hissing noise confirmed his suspicion.

He set off dead slow again.

By his fourth lap, he was much more confident. He no longer had to walk like Frankenstein's monster in case he bumped into a ladder.

This is why he was surprised when he kicked something metallic.

Bats evacuated a tree with a noisy shriek as the thing clattered in front of him.

James swore loudly as he staggered to regain his balance. "Damn!"

He realised he had just kicked over the open paint tin they had forgotten to pack away.

He turned around and hobbled to the front door.

———

"That you, Jimbo?" Oodles shouted from the lounge when James staggered into the house and slammed the door behind him.

"Who else were you expecting?" James said.

The door to the lounge-room opened and Oodles's head appeared. "What was that noise about?"

"I think I kicked one of the damn paint tins over in the dark."

James sat down on the chair in the hall, removed his left shoe and rubbed his foot.

"Strewth!" Oodles smacked his forehead. "I told you blokes to remind me we still had to clean up."

"I think I just did." James winced.

"Bit late now. I hate to think of the mess you've just made."

James glared at him. "I could have killed myself! You would have had a bigger mess to clean up then."

———

James thought reading the final dozen pages of *Far from the Madding Crowd* might help him calm down.

But when he sank back on to his bed, he realised it was like trying to read Egyptian hieroglyphs through frosted glass. He went over passages again and again, but they made no sense.

Messerschmitt kept intruding on his thoughts. How was he going to get that thug out of his house? And how was he going to stand up in court and testify against him when he was glaring at him from the dock?

He got up from the bed and hobbled over to the window, intending to open it and clear his head with an infusion of fresh air.

As he approached, he noticed he had left the back light on.

Then he saw them.

A pair of eyes looked back at him from the edge of the bushland.

They were eyes full of hate.

James went numb. He struggled to breathe. His chest felt like a heavy weight had suddenly descended on it.

His evil nephew was standing at the edge of the garden wearing a surgical mask, and thumping a baseball bat against his thigh.

NINETEEN
KILLER TRACKS

JAMES LOOKED DOWN at the paw-prints left in the spilled green paint. "Another one of your pranks, Bert?"

It was the morning after his encounter in the dark with the paint tin.

Wish-Wash got down on one knee to inspect the marks. "Nothing to do with me, Jimbo." He shook his head. "But I've seen tracks like these before."

Oodles peered over his shoulder. "Are you sure, old son?"

"Of course I'm flamin' sure. I reckon we should get Moose up here A.S.A.P.. He'll want to know a Tasmanian Tiger is prowling around this neighbourhood."

"Oh, for goodness sake," James said. "You really do think I came down in the last shower."

As if on cue, the heavens opened up. It wasn't the drizzle Windy Mountain often got. It was a violent downburst.

"Quick." Oodles started gathering the tins, including the upturned one James had kicked over. "Let's pick up what we can and get inside."

Little green rivers were already forming on the ground, washing away the animal tracks.

A downpipe clanged and gurgled.

James picked up the plastic ice-cream container. The brushes in the container bobbled in a rapidly rising sea, which was more water than turps now.

"Just tip it all out on the ground," Oodles said over the noise of the downpour. "What's a bit more green pa—"

He stopped short when he realised Wish-Wash wasn't helping. He looked around at the same time James did to see Wish-Wash had stepped back under the eaves and was looking down at his white handkerchief.

A bead of water hung off the end of one of his nostrils and his blue singlet had turned two-tone with streaks of rain.

"What?" Wish-Wash shouted when he realised he was the target of their glares. "I'm just making my rain hat. Is that OK?"

"Really, Bert!" James screamed. "The least you can do is help. You did contribute to this mess last night."

Wish-Wash continued making his handkerchief hat. "You're very loose with your accusations, Jimbo. I was no where near this place last night. Besides, you blokes are wearing overalls. It doesn't matter how wet you get."

James squeezed the brushes as he poured out the pale green diluted turps. "I don't know how you did it, Bert, because I was awake half the night knowing Messerschmitt was standing in the garden, but you must have sneaked out here at some point to make those animal tracks."

"Why don't you believe me?" Wish-Wash planted his knotted handkerchief hat on his head.

James stood up. "I would have to believe the Tasmanian Tiger really still existed to believe you."

———

When they got inside, they made a beeline for the bathroom to towel themselves off. It was the first time they had all been in that room at the same time.

"You know you're still wearing your handkerchief hat, old son?" Oodles said, as they jostled for position.

Wish-Wash checked himself in the mirror. "So I am. I bet you blokes wished you had thought of this."

"You do realise you look like a pillock, Bert?" James said.

"At least I am a dry pillock. You blokes look like drowned rats."

Wish-Wash unknotted the corners of his soggy handkerchief and returned it to his pocket.

James saw the look of discomfort on his face as moisture was most likely seeping through to his skin.

They paraded back into the living room in single file.

Oodles went into the kitchen and James could hear him stoking the stove with the poker, then the radio came on.

"Close that lounge-room door, someone," Oodles called out. "We don't want to let the heat out today."

When he reappeared, he was carrying a cardboard box, which he plonked down onto the table.

The writing on the side said it was a dinner set.

But when Wish-Wash peered in through the top he became excited when he realised it didn't actually contain plates.

"Where did you find the other videos?"

"Under my bed," Oodles said.

"When?"

"The morning after you found the other video. I realised then where I hadn't looked."

Wish-Wash frowned. "How come the box was in the kitchen if you found it under the bed?"

"I was hiding them in the crockery cupboard, somewhere I knew you'd never look, old son?"

"Why would you keep them a secret in the first place?"

"I was saving them for a rainy day like this. No offence, but I'm getting a bit tired of Scrabble."

Wish-Wash rifled around the box, clacking the videos from side to side. "One . . . two . . . three . . . four . . . five . . . six . . . seven . . . eight of them. None of them are marked. Didn't your missus believe in putting labels on things?"

Oodles looked into the middle-distance. "I guess she had her own filing system."

"Do you reckon they're the full set of Janey Fondas?" Wish-Wash said. "

"Oh, for goodness sake," James grumbled. "You do not expect me to watch any more of that nonsense? That jigsaw Maddie left me might even be a better alternative."

"I've got another idea," Wish-Wash said. "While we're watching the videos, you can play Scrabble on your own, Jimbo. It'll help you work out where you've been going wrong?"

"Work out how to cheat like you, you mean," James snarled as he stepped towards him.

Oodles stepped between them. "Look, if you two can't get on, one of you is going to have to go outside in the rain."

"It is not going to be me," James said. "Bert is the one who likes sneaking outside."

"For the last time, it wasn't me." Wish-Wash held out an open palm, then sighed, then couldn't keep a straight face any more
. "OK, I'll come clean. That Tasmanian Tiger you saw out your bedroom window *was* a prank I cooked up with Moose and Joffa."

James slapped a thigh. "I knew it!"

Wish-Wash smirked. "You were fooled by a fibreglass ornament Moose and Joffa found in Chalky le Blanc's garden while we were in Ireland." He puffed out his chest. "They parked their ute at the bottom of the hill and had a hell of a job carrying it up, but it was worth it to see the look on your face the next morning!"

James hissed. "Just listen to yourself, Bert! Now you are taking credit for carrying it up the hill."

"I'm the one who came up with the flamin' idea, didn't I?" Wish-Wash said. "I'm the one who told them which part of the garden would be best for it. I'm the one who left the back light on."

James turned around to Oodles. "Did you know about this, Clarence?"

Oodles started stammering, but Wish-Wash spoke over him. "Who do you think came up with the idea to put the mask on the flamin' tiger? Anyway, it had nothing to do with what we saw at the side of the house. Those paw prints were the real McCoy."

TWENTY
DISSECTOLOGIST REVEALS HIMSELF

JAMES STARTED SORTING the jigsaw pieces into piles according to their colours on the yellow laminate table.

"Do you know what you're doing over there, old son?" Oodles asked as he sat back in his chair waiting for Wish-Wash to start the first of the videos.

"Oh, please!" James said. "How hard could it be? You are talking to a man who used to have rooms of angry ratepayers eating out of his hand."

"Did you ever have 1000 ratepayers at a time?"

"What's your point, Clarence?"

"Isn't that how many jigsaw pieces you've got there?"

"Are you doubting my abilities?"

"Noooooooooooo," Wish-Wash cried, and James and Oodles looked his way.

The big man was staring at the screen, white-lipped with anger.

"Who tapes games of lawn bowls and keeps them so long?" he said.

"I told you they were likely to be pirated recordings of *Jack High*, old cock," Oodles said. "But you can't blame Madge for keeping them so long. She hadn't banked on dying."

Wish-Wash loped towards the VCR with another tape in hand. "They can't all be of flamin' lawn bowls."

That's where he was wrong. Again and again!

James found it hard to concentrate with Wish-Wash's escalating moaning and groaning every time he put in a tape and found it was another episode of *Jack High*.

Just to be sure Jane Fonda wasn't lurking on any of the videos, Wish-Wash gave them all a second run through. He fast-forwarded and stopped-started each tape to make sure lawn bowls wasn't the only thing on there. It was hard to know if the whirring and whining noises were coming from the video player or Bert.

On top of this, every hour James's fitness tracker vibrated on his wrist to demand 250 more steps.

The only way to keep it happy was to do laps up and down the draughty hallway.

Oodles glared at him every time he opened the door and let out the heat, but Wish-Wash couldn't resist having a laugh. "Running to the dunny again, Jimbo? Don't forget to wash your hands."

"I thought you were searching for a hussy in a leotard? You know fine-well I am doing my laps indoors, so I am out of he weather, Bert."

"I don't even know why you're still wearing that thing." Wish-Wash pointed to the top of the china cabinet where the green and blue bands sat next to the pile of masks. "Oodles and I got rid of ours ages ago. Bad enough you're spying on us, who knows who else is stealing our data?"

"So you think the Chinese might be listening in, Bert? Or Wikileaks? Get real, man." He slammed the door behind him.

When he returned, James sat down sullenly and examined some jigsaw pieces looking for a rooftop.

He thought Wish-Wash's focus had returned to the videos but he heard the words: "I would never have picked you for a dissectologist, Jimbo?"

James looked up and frowned. "A what?"

"A dissectologist." Wish-Wash smiled. "It's someone who enjoys jigsaw puzzle assembly."

"You just made that up, just like you make up words in Scrabble."

Wish-Wash shook his head. "You think you're the only one who knows big words? Sucked in! I told you my set of encyclopaedias would come in handy."

James put his head down again, and went into ignore mode.

He didn't look up until almost lunchtime.

By then, the jigsaw was coming along well.

The Arc de Triomphe was taking shape, as were the surrounding Parisian rooftops. The Eiffel Tower was missing only two pieces.

He hadn't started on the Champs-Elysees yet because he knew that would incorporate actual cyclists but he was approaching that juncture.

He was deep in thought when a shrill whistle pierced the room.

TWENTY-ONE
GOING POSTAL

Oodles got up from his armchair and walked over to the Venetian blinds.

He lifted a slat. "It's Gus Foot again. He's parked by the gate and he's holding a letter."

Wish-Wash stopped his fast-forwarding. "In the rain?"

Oodles squinted out. "Looks like it's stopped."

"How did Gus make that whistling sound?" Wish-Wash asked.

Oodles looked out again, then shrugged. "I guess he put two fingers in his mouth and blew. Some people are good at that."

He turned around in time for Wish-Wash to say: "I'm not. It's about the only thing stopping me from applying for a job as a postie. I reckon I'd be really good though at carrying off the colourful uniform they wear these days."

"Oh, and you'd be fine handling a motorbike, would you?" Oodles said.

"I didn't say that." Wish-Wash scratched a hairy shoulder that stuck out from the side of his blue singlet. "I reckon a lot of people would love to return to the days when posties used to walk around the streets, and make deliveries twice a day. Remember them times?

Nothing gave you a bigger buzz than the sound of a whistle from the postie letting you know they had just left a letter in your box."

Oodles looked into the middle-distance again. "Why do you reckon they don't do that any more?"

"Cost-cutting probably," Wish-Wash said.

Oodles looked hard at him.

"You think about it. We must have had thousands of posties in those days, tens of thousands to cover this big country. Most were on foot, the lucky buggers on bicycles, but one thing they had in common is they all were equipped with whistles. The beancounters — or in this case, the pea-counters" — he laughed at his joke — "would have had a field day saving all that money by getting rid of the whistles."

"You reckon?" Oodles said. "Who would they have sold them to?"

"Hmm, good question," Wish-Wash said. "No e-Bay in those days, was there? Hmm, I'll need to think about it."

James stood up abruptly. "Oh, for heavens sake! Is there any danger of anyone actually going outside to get the letter?"

"Nice of you to volunteer, old son," Oodles said.

"It's not even my house," James muttered as he turned the doorknob.

———

Gus looked surprised to see James. "How did you know this is for you?"

"For me? Again?" James took the letter and examined it on both sides. Not only did it not have a return address, it didn't carry a stamp.

"Well?" Gus said. "Aren't you going to open it? The suspense is killing me." His helmet was hanging from a strap from the handlebars. "It's the only reason I've been waiting so long."

James looked him up and down. It wasn't raining now but his yellow oilskins were glistening and the spikes on his motorbike wheels were splattered with mud. "How long have you been waiting at the gate?"

"A good 10 minutes," Gus said. "Maybe more. I knew you were hard of hearing but I thought Wishy or Oodles would have heard me wolf-whistling."

"Oh, they did," James said. "It's just they got a little sidetracked. You know what they're like? They're away with the fairies most of the time." He quickly added: "You won't tell them I said that about them, will you?"

"Of course not," Gus said. "I'm good at keeping secrets. You should hear what they say about you!"

James swallowed, then waved the letter. "Are you even supposed to deliver letters that haven't got stamps?"

"Technically, no," Gus said. "But we also get into trouble if we return to the depot with a letter left in our saddlebags."

"I see. And this letter was in your saddlebags?" James said.

Gus shook his head. "Yes, but the odd thing is I didn't notice when I was filling it up in the sorting room."

James refocused on the envelope. "You sure? No one else could have slipped it in the bags?"

"Why would they do that?" Gus said.

"A good question." James picked a cotton from his overalls.

"You think someone who doesn't like me is trying to get me into trouble?"

"Maybe you are not as likeable as you thought? I seem to recall your gang deserted you all those years ago."

Gus gave him a leader-of-the pack glare. He was Foetus once more. "That was a misunderstanding and you know it." He banged a hand on the handlebars as he spoke. The metal clanged every time his skull-ring connected. "Are you going to open that fucking envelope, or not?"

————

The letter inside was unsigned.

James knew immediately who it was from though.

His hands trembled as he looked down at the three scribbled words.

I'm watching you

"You all right, Jimbo?" Gus said. "You've gone all pale."

"You'd be pale, too, if you had seen Messerschmitt standing in the garden with a baseball bat, and now you've received this letter from him." James turned the note towards Gus so he could read it.

Gus's eyes widened as he examined it. "I thought Messy was back in jail."

"No, he's staying at my place."

"Your place? Aren't you down to give evidence against him?"

"How do you know that?"

"Contacts." Gus tapped his nose. "In my business, it pays to know who's doing what to whom. You never know when a piece of intel will come in handy."

"Well, store this tidbit away. Not only is Messerschmitt living in my house without my permission, now he's trying to intimidate me."

Gus snatched the letter from James and studied it. "I'm watching you Is that all it says?"

"It's a clear threat," James said.

"You obviously haven't been in as many courtrooms as me. His lawyer wouldn't even have to be particularly smart to convince a jury that's not actually a threat. It hasn't even got a full stop. He might have posted it accidentally without even finishing it."

James snatched back the letter. "So how did this get into your mailbags?"

"Beats me," Gus said. "Way I see it there were two opportunities. Either someone at the post office slipped it in there overnight before I even got to work, which, as I said, is unlikely, or someone put it in there while I was answering a call of nature at the public toilets at the Recreation Ground."

James gasped. "You left your motorbike unguarded outside the public toilets?"

"What would you have me do? Drag 250ccs into Cubicle Two with me?"

James mopped his brow with his handkerchief. "Good grief! How long were you in there?"

"Dunno." Gus looked up to swaying treetops nearby and pondered. "I don't usually have trouble with *The Pick of the Crop*'s crosswords but I got stuck with 12 down, 15 across today. How did you go?"

"As if I read the local rag!"

"Isn't your son-in-law the editor?"

"That's another good reason not to read it," James said. "Besides, none of this rings true. How can you do their crossword when the paper's solely online?"

Gus reached into his saddlebags, pulled out a large tablet computer and prodded it with a finger. "Marvel of modern technology. It's not so clever as a backup if the bog paper runs out though."

James tossed his head back. It was too much information. "What I want to know is did you notice anyone suspicious when you came out?"

Gus gazed at the treetops again. "Two boys were kicking a football back and forwards on the oval, and I saw the back of a bloke walking a dog across the other side. Other than that, nothing."

James began to shake. "I don't know what to do. It's not like I can even go into hiding. Messerschmitt knows where I live — and will have to continue to live until I come out of isolation hell."

Gus stroked his beard. "I see your problem, Jimbo. Good thing for you Messerschmitt is the one man in this town I like less than you."

"What's that supposed to mean?"

"It means I know some blokes who can make this problem go away for you."

"Go away?"

Gus smiled. "Messerschmitt will find it hard standing in your garden with two broken legs."

"You're not serious?"

"This is your lucky day. The people I know are offering some good deals because business is slow with most people in lockdown. Normally it'd cost you $500 a limb but for $900 you can get the buy-one-break-one-free deal. Two arms, two legs. How good is that? In the spirit of the sale, I'll even halve my 20 per cent facilitator's fee."

"You'd charge me?"

"A man's gotta earn enough to eat. It's a basic human right."

"I couldn't possibly condone violence," James spluttered. "A man of my position can't afford to put his reputation at risk! Messerschmitt would just love turning the legal-aid hounds on me."

"Believe me, he'd never feel safe testifying against you. I know blokes like that. They can dish it up but they can't take it. The guys I contract will have him crying for his mother."

James closed his eyes. "That's another problem. His mother is my sister. I couldn't do that to her. If all his limbs were broken, think of the things she'd have to do for him."

"In that case, Jimbo, you have no choice but to go for the final solution." Gus drew a finger across his throat.

"You have to be joking!"

"What else are you going to do? You think asking him politely to go away will do any good?"

"But, good grief, I could never go that far."

"Why not? They'd never be able to track it back to you. The blokes I know are professionals." Gus pulled his mobile phone from his pocket, and called up a site on the dark web. "Wow, that's an amazing deal." He looked up at James. "For $10,000 they'll break every bone in his body and drop him down an old mine shaft somewhere on the West Coast. He'd never be seen again."

"Where would I even get $10,000?" James screeched.

"You forget. I'm an investment adviser. Stockbrokers talk. $10,000 is a drop in the ocean for you. Which reminds me, these hitmen don't always use mine shafts. Sometimes they go on a boat trip and submerge the corpses with lead weights. It depends what they have planned for the weekend. Some hitmen like to relax with a bit of fishing."

James closed his eyes. "I couldn't possibly go through with this."

"Way I see it you'd be a fool not to." Gus called up Google and lodged a query. "Interesting. Did you know there are 207 bones in the human body?"

He switched to calculator mode and punched in some numbers with his meaty fingers. "If you were paying $500 for each bone, that would cost you $103,500 — plus my commission."

He put in some more numbers, then looked up. "Wow! With this deal, you'd only be paying $48.3 per bone."

Gus refused to take no for an answer, and suggested James sleep on it.

He'd speak to his contacts as soon as James gave the word.

TWENTY-TWO
JIGSORE

WHEN JAMES RETURNED to the living room, his jigsaw was gone. It had been replaced on the yellow formica table by three soup bowls and a stick of French bread.

"Lunch won't be long," Oodles called from the kitchen. "I'm just heating up that seafood chowder Katy left for us. We only have yesterday's bread sticks but we can always toast them."

James was still processing what had just happened outside, now he felt doubly numb.

As he stared gape-mouthed at the table, he became aware that Wish-Wash now looking over his shoulder.

"I hope you didn't mind," Wish-Wash said. "Oodles asked me to set the table, and there just wasn't enough room for the plates and your jigsaw puzzle."

"I see," James said flatly.

Wish-Wash stepped into view. "You're not angry?" He looked disappointed.

"Worse things happen at sea." As soon as James said that, he regretted saying it. He had a mental image of Messerschmitt's battered corpse being fitted out with weights on the deck of a boat.

"Are you all right, Jimbo?" Wish-Wash pointed to the top of the china cabinet. "I put all the pieces back in the box up there. A thousand of them. You can count them if you like."

"I trust you, Bert," James said.

"You're really not feeling well, are you?"

————

"Who would have thought we'd be eating seafood chowder in Windy Mountain?" Wish-Wash said between slurps. 'It's just like we're together in Ireland again."

Oodles balanced a Tiger prawn on his spoon. "I can't remember getting prawns and scallops in the chowder over there though. All I remember is getting cod and the odd mussel."

Wish-Wash put down his spoon and ripped off a piece of the bread stick. He dunked it three times in the soup and raised it to his mouth, sending small drops flying across the table. But instead of consuming it whole, he started sucking the end until he was satisfied he had got all the liquid. Only then did he finish the bread off.

Flecks of bread sprayed from his mouth as he spoke. "So, that letter was actually for you, Jimbo? Who was it from?"

James dabbed his face with his napkin. "No one really?"

Oodles stopped sipping and suspended his spoon in mid-air. "No one? It had to be from someone."

"It was not even for me. Wrong address," James said.

"Wrong address?" Wish-Wash frowned. "You'd think Gus would have known."

"He says he's legally bound to deliver his letters to the address on the envelope," James said.

"You learn something new every day." Oodles dipped his spoon once more.

"How come you were out there for so long?" Wish-Wash sprayed more bread as he spoke.

"Pardon?" James said.

"You were out at the gate for yonks," Wish-Wash said.

"If you must know, it was nice talking to someone other than you two."

"I get that," Oodles said. "But Gus strikes me as an unlikely substitute for you to have a long chinwag with. I wouldn't have thought you had much in common?"

"So what did you talk about?" Wish-Wash said.

"You're not the only one who has secrets, Bert."

"No need to get snarky. I was just trying to make polite conversation."

James rested his spoon back down next to his place-mat and pushed his bowl away. It was still two-thirds full.

"Don't you want that?" Wish-Wash said. "Because if you don't, my name's on it."

James sighed. "Go for your life, Bert. I'm guessing globs of your DNA are already in it anyway."

"There is no need to be rude, Jimbo," Wish-Wash said, dragging the bowl towards him. Then he turned and addressed Oodles. "I've been mulling it over. I think I can make an educated guess about what happened to all those whistles?"

"They sold them all back to China?"

Wish-Wash scoffed. "Things like that were all made in Japan back then. The Japs wouldn't have wanted all our Aussie germs."

"So what do you think happened to them?" Oodles asked.

"I reckon they put them where no taxman would ever be able to find them."

"Where?" Oodles asked.

"I reckon they bunged them all into a tip truck and poured them down a deserted mineshaft."

————

Oodles said he had just the thing for James to set his jigsaw up on permanently.

"Don't worry about it, Clarence." James said. He was finding it hard to just breathe.

"Nonsense. It's in the garage. I'll go and get it."

When Oodles disappeared out the door, Wish-Wash said: "It's for the best, Jimbo. The main table doesn't have enough room."

"The thing is I might never have the inclination to complete a jigsaw again."

Wish-Wash stared down at him, his nostrils flaring like a bull. "You didn't complete that flamin' one. Lots of pieces were missing."

"I would have knocked it over this afternoon."

"You still can now." Wish-Wash prodded his own chest. "No need to thank me for making it easier for you."

"Easier?"

"You know where a lot of the pieces go now."

Oodles walked in through the doorway carrying a folded-up card table. He had rain drops on his overalls. "The downpour has started again with a vengeance. We'll be lucky to get any painting done for the rest of the week. This weather looks like it's set in."

"Hear that, Jimbo?" Wish-Wash said. "You'll have more time to do your jigsaw and do laps of the hallway pretending you're Cadel Evans."

"Who?"

"You don't actually know anything about cycling, do you?" Wish-Wash said.

"And you do, I suppose, being one of the world's great know-alls?"

"I know the name of the only Aussie to have won the race and I once owned a bicycle. So put that in your pipe and smoke it!"

"My exercise in the hall has nothing to do with cyclists, Bert, and you know it." James put a hand on the left side of his groin. "It's not that many weeks ago they shoved a wire up my femoral artery so they could position a stent in my heart. It's crucial I keep up my exercise now. Especially now, with that hooligan putting my blood pressure up again."

"Are you saying Oodles and I don't exercise?"

"You've abandoned the fitness trackers Maddie bought you!"

"I'm supposed to feel ashamed, am I? That girl of yours said a while back I looked like a cow."

James scratched his head. "What's that got to do with this?"

"There was nothing wrong with my black and white camouflage trousers." Wish-Wash looked to Oodles for support. "Was there, cobber?"

"Will you blokes cut it out," Oodles said. "I need to get this table set up pronto before we can watch Jane Fonda."

James pinched the bridge of his nose. "Oh, my Lord, you found another one?"

Wish-Wash stuck out his bottom lip. "Unfortunately, no. Every single one of those videos in the box were of lawn bowls. You believe that? I fast-forwarded through the last one while you were out not getting a letter." He blew out his cheeks. "We've got no choice but to watch the first Janey video from the beginning."

TWENTY-THREE
THE GREEN, GREEN PRINTS OF HOME

OODLES SET up the card table with the green-felt top in the space between the two TVs.

"That is not going to work," James complained. "I need peace and quiet. Can you not put it in my bedroom?"

"You'd freeze your proverbials off in there, old son," Oodles said. "Besides, there's not room in that shoebox. You'd have to take the bed out."

This was true but the reality was there was not much spare room in here any more either. One sofa, two armchairs, one full-sized table, one TV that worked only with a video player, one TV that did not work at all, one china cabinet and three old blokes.

The close proximity of the working TV screen was very distracting.

Wish-Wash, now topless, was smiling smugly when he slid in the Jane Fonda workout video, pressed play and took five steps back, his man-boobs wobbling.

He stood there, hands on hips, as he waited for something to happen. As the blank screen persisted, his face cycled through a number of emotions — bewilderment, concern then despair.

Being seated so close, and with his hearing aids switched up, James was probably the first to work out why the video machine wasn't working. The scrunching noise unlocked a memory. It was eating the tape bit by bit, sucking it into the works. Yes, he recalled now. It didn't pay to play a lot of old tapes without running a video-heads cleaning tape to remove the build-up of oxide.

It was likely Wish-Wash now remembered, too. He rushed towards the video screaming: "Noooooooooo."

———

Wish-Wash sat cross-legged on the floor inspecting the twisted, broken tape. He had tugged it so hard to pull it out of the works, he had snapped it.

He looked like he was about to cry as he held up two pieces. "Do you reckon I can glue these back together?"

"Give it up, old cock," Oodles said.

Just then, the doorbell rang.

Ding-dong, ding-dong.

Wish-Wash brightened. "Maybe it's Awesome Sauce. He'd know what to do?"

"You really are dreaming," Oodles said. "Why would he come here? And even if it is him, what makes you think he'd have a blinking clue? He'd know as much about VHS players as we'd know about Model T Fords."

James looked up from the Eiffel Tower. "Hey! My father had a Model T Ford."

"Exactly," Oodles said. "And Awesome Sauce's father probably had a VHS player. Fat lot of good that is."

The doorbell rang again.

Ding-dong, ding-dong.

"Who do you think it is?" James asked.

"It's too early for Katy. It must be for you, old son," Oodles said.

"Me? How do you work that out?"

Wish-Wash looked up from his tangle. "It's a mystery to us, too, why you've become so popular."

James exhaled heavily as he stood up. "Where are the masks," he said as he started walking towards the door.

"Where they always are," Oodles said. "On top of the china cabinet."

James took his off the top of the pile. He knew it was his because he had now marked his with a marking pen.

The bell rang again just as he was opening the door.

Conn was standing there again.

"I tink you need to know dis," he blurted. "Your cousin left the house last night."

"Tell me something I don't know," James muffled through his mask.

"He came back," Conn said.

James ripped off the mask. "You let him back in?"

"No, I had already gone to bed. He let himself in with the spare key he had taken from the hook in the kitchen."

James rolled his eyes.

"But it's worse than dat," Conn said.

"Worse?"

"He brought Eva in with him," Conn said.

"His girlfriend?"

"No, his German Shepherd."

James winced. "I thought his dog was called Adolf?"

Conn shrugged. "I'm pretty sure he called her Eva. It's not the first time she's been inside either. It was the only way we could get her to stop digging holes in your garden."

James's face crumpled.

"Dis was the first time she had left green paw prints on the carpet though."

TWENTY-FOUR
THE CANTANKEROUS OLD COOT OF MONTE CRISTO
EIGHT WEEKS IN

He smiled to himself as he marked off the date on the calendar hanging from his bedroom wall.

This was indeed a day to savour. It was his 83rd birthday.

James stroked the point of his chin with his thumb and forefinger as he studied the calendar. His overnight stubble make a light rasping noise.

This was his fifty-seventh day imprisoned in this cultural vacuum — but the end was in sight. He only had to endure four more weeks of self-isolation.

Liberation day would mean the end of Scrabble. No more culture-less jigsaw puzzles. No more peasant food. No more appalling table manners. No more childish pranks. He would never have to slap cheap green paint on to weatherboards again.

All he had to do now was figure out how to shift Messerschmitt out of his cottage so he could resume the comforts of his home.

James ran his hand over his stubble again, and liked the rasping sound it made. He hadn't missed a day of shaving in 65 years but perhaps it was time to start cultivating the Edmond Dantès bearded look.

James had become reacquainted with Dantès via the old e-reader Conn Northan had brought him.

James didn't know where Conn had even found that slow, old thing — probably in a drawer where he had most likely tucked it away after his new e-reader had arrived.

It pained him to have to read some of those books again — but *The Count of Monte Cristo* seemed appropriate.

Published in 1844, Dantès is imprisoned in the infamous Château d'If, where the most dangerous political prisoners are kept. James felt a kinship. He guessed he would have got the same treatment, being a former mayor.

Dantès uses the broken handle of a pot to scratch away the stone wall of his cell while his neighbour is scratching away at his side. Eventually, they break through and he meets an Italian priest and intellectual, who teaches him history, science and philosophy. The priest also tells Dantès about a treasure hidden on the island of Monte Cristo. When the priest dies, Dantès hides himself in his shroud, which is thrown into the sea from a great height. Dantès cuts himself loose and swims to freedom. Onwards to the treasure!

In his moments of despair, James thought about breaking through to the next room, too.

But he quickly dismissed it when he returned to reality and remembered the man in the adjoining bedroom was Wish-Wash, whose only knowledge of science was narrowly focused pre-1963 and whose idea of treasure was the bargain rack at the Slutz Plains Op Shop.

James stepped over to the window.

It looked like they were in for a nice day for a change.

It had rained almost non-stop for the past week.

This had stopped the painting work, which was a good thing. The downside was it gave them time to play yet more Scrabble and give each other haircuts. He had almost completed the Champs-Elysées jigsaw on the card table, too.

The drizzle hadn't stopped Messerschmitt standing in the garden each night.

James had no doubt Messerschmitt had helped himself to that expensive black umbrella from the rack in the cottage porch.

He was always gone by daylight. And nothing had actually happened.

James focused on the Hill's Hoist in the middle of the lawn. Wish-Wash's orange and swirly green tracksuit pants were hanging on the line again.

———

"Happy birthday, Jimbo." Wish-Wash looked up from the toaster when James walked into the kitchen.

He was wearing his blue singlet. But this time he was wearing traffic-light red trousers.

James was pretty sure he had seen these trousers before, only on a different man.

Wish-Wash began lathering his toast with large globs of butter. "So, do you have anything to say to me?"

"Yes. Aren't they Rod's trousers you're wearing?"

"I didn't mean that." Wish-Wash shook his head as he started layering Vegemite on top of the butter. "I meant it's your turn to wish *me* happy birthday."

James was flabbergasted. "Since when did you celebrate your birthday the same day as me?"

"Other way around, I'd reckon. You wouldn't even have been a twinkle in your father's eye when I was born 84 years ago."

"What I mean, Bert, is how come I've never known about this? They made a big deal out of birthdays when we were at primary school together."

Wish-Wash looked up and gazed at the wall. "They did, didn't they? But I wasn't about to draw attention to the fact I was a year older than everyone else because I had been kept back a year. Besides, if you declared it was your birthday, kids would expect you to invite them to your party. My mum never had money for parties, only rich kids did that."

He turned and his eyes were full of fury. "I haven't forgotten that year when you invited every boy in the class to your party, except me."

"The invitation probably got lost in the mail."

Wish-Wash gave a little laugh. "Don't you flamin' remember? You handed them out personally."

James opened his mouth but no words came out.

"Doesn't matter," Wish-Wash said. "I wouldn't have come anyway. We couldn't afford presents."

"Yes . . . well . . . happy birthday, Bert. I wish though you had told me sooner. You know how to embarrass a man."

"You're right about these trousers, by the way," Wish-Wash said. "I couldn't believe my luck when I came across them on the rack at the Slutz Plains Op Shop. My grandson must have traded them in before he went on the Elvis tour."

"Why would he have done that?"

Wish-Wash picked up his toast and began biting into it. He got most of it in his mouth, but small golden and black lava flows were running down his chin by the time he could talk. "Maybe they have a dress code. Perhaps he has to wear one of the white jumpsuits too?"

"He's driving the bus. He's not one of the Elvis impersonators?"

Wish-Wash shrugged. "All I know is these trousers have come back to me. When I traded them in for my orange and swirly green trackie-dackies, I was sad because I never expected to see them in my wardrobe again."

———

Wish-Wash opened the enamel door of the speckled-green stove and put in another log, poked the fire and turned on the radio. Then they moved to the adjoining room where the table was already laid with boxes of cereal, a carton of milk, a bowl of sugar, cutlery and crockery.

Oodles shuffled into the living room. He was wearing blue slippers with his beige overalls. "If it isn't the birthday boys! Many happy returns to you both."

James gasped. "You knew it was *his* birthday, too?"

Oodles sat down and reached for the Weetbix. "Of course I knew. Didn't you?"

"Bert has just told me." James glanced over the table at the big man. "Didn't you?"

Wish-Wash nodded and started pouring coco-pops into a bowl.

James stopped eating his cereal. "What are you doing?"

Wish-Wash spooned sugar on to the coco-pops, then poured milk in the bowl. "What does it look like I'm doing?"

"You've already had your toast!"

"I was hungry."

"The done thing is to eat your cereal *before* eating your toast."

Wish-Wash glanced across to Oodles. "It all goes down the same way, doesn't it cobber? My stomach isn't going to worry about the order it comes in."

Oodles nodded towards James. "It doesn't worry me any more than you not shaving, old son."

James swept a hand down his cheek. "Is it that obvious?"

"It's no big deal to me if you shave before or after brekky. If it's so wrong eating your cereal out of order, how come Wish-Wash made it to all these years."

"Yes," Wish-Wash agreed. "So, go plait your poop, Greybeard."

"Now, now," Oodles pointed his spoon from man to man. "This isn't a day you two blokes should be bickering. I've got a special surprise coming for both of you."

———

When they opened the front door, the first thing James saw was the birthday cake on a table that had been set up at the bottom of the three steps. The cake was aglow with what he assumed were 167 flickering candles.

A woman with pink hair was standing on the other side of the gate.

When she looked up from her phone, he realised it was Wendy Bennett from the Wind Tunnel Cafe.

"This is not my natural colour, I'll have you know," she said in her gravelly voice to no one in particular.

Wish-Wash shot back. "What is your real colour, Wendy? Grey?"

"Just sit down before I take that bloody cake back," she said in her 30-cigarettes-a-day voice.

The table sat 10 yards from the fence. A yellow china teapot and three cups and saucers completed the settings. Plastic chairs stood at three sides.

"It's not my fault the local hairdresser is shut down," Wendy said, "and this was the only do-it-yourself colour the supermarket is selling. It's not just me. Every second woman you pass in the High Street has pink hair. Anyway, you blokes can't go on about bad hair-do's. Have any of you looked in a mirror?"

Her voice dropped. "Is this what you wanted, Oodles? It took me ages to light all those candles. Better blow them out quickly, before the wind gets them."

Wish-Wash took a deep breath, but James's hand shot out and covered his mouth. "Don't you dare," he hissed.

Wish-Wash looked hurt. "Why not?"

"Germs."

"It's fun to blow out the candles on a birthday cake. Come on, we can do it together."

James was already plucking the candles out of the cake one by one and throwing them on to the ground next to his seat.

"Spoilsport," Wish-Wash said, looking to Oodles for support.

"He's probably right, old son," Oodles said. "No telling who's stickybeaking out their windows. We don't want to break the law, especially at the moment."

"One hundred and sixty-seven times," James added. "People expect people like me to set an example."

Wendy croaked: "It's your favourite, Wish-Wash. A strawberry cheesecake on a base of crushed chocolate digestive biscuits."

"But it's for both of you," Oodles added quickly. "It's my present to both of you." He looked up at Wendy. "Isn't that right?"

Wendy nodded. "If my best customers can't come to the cafe, the cafe must come to them."

Wish-Wash grabbed the big knife. "Shall I be mother?"

Oodles wrested the handle from him. "You can pour the tea. I'll cut the cake."

Wendy giggled until she started coughing. When she had recovered from her fits of hacking, she said: "You old blokes haven't changed a bit in isolation, I see." She peered above their heads and admired the shiny, new paint. "So it's true? You've been busy painting?"

"Who told you that?" Oodles asked, as he hovered over the cake.

Wendy shrugged. "I overheard customers talking."

"Why would anyone be interested in what we're doing up here?"

"You'd be surprised, love. I heard someone is running a book on whether you'll all last the distance together."

Oodles looked down at the cake to make sure he was cutting straight. "None of us is allowed to kick the bucket until the painting is done. It's bad enough the weather is conspiring against us. We've virtually come to a halt this past week."

"So you decided to do some hair-cutting during the downtime, eh?" Wendy started laugh-hacking again.

Oodles shook his head as he lifted a slice of cake on to Wish-Wash's plate. "We probably should have waited for four more weeks and gone to Katy, but it'll grow back."

"Is that why Jimbo is growing a beard? To compensate?"

"Will you quit it," James said. "Is a man not allowed to have a rest from his razor on his birthday? No one says anything about Bert missing weeks at a time."

Wendy looked up at the cloudless sky. "So you'll be back into the painting today?"

Oodles served a slab of cake to James. "Too muddy. Besides, you can't expect these blokes to work on their birthdays. I'd be on my Pat Malone."

"I know the feeling." Wendy twiddled strands of her hair. "My place is getting a bit tatty now Gordo isn't around. The cafe needs a fresh coat of paint, but I wouldn't even know where to start."

Oodles served himself a slice and tested it with a lick of his thumb. "Nice cake. Tell you what. Once we're out of this isolation, we'd be happy to help out." He looked from face to face. "Wouldn't we, boys?"

James nearly choked as he lifted his fork to his lips. Did he just hear right? He had just been volunteered! "I do hope you like the colour green, Wendy?"

"Why green?" Wendy frowned.

"You'll find out."

"That reminds me, Jimbo," Wendy said. "I've just been on the phone to Moose. He'll deliver your present from the Lady Mayor this afternoon."

James opened his eyes wide. "What present?"

"Maddie didn't tell you? I guess it's a secret then."

"Why's that ruffian delivering it?"

Wendy shrugged. "Moose's got a ute. And I think he's bringing that American kid with the pimples to help him set the present up."

James looked at his table-mates, hoping for a clue what it all was.

"Don't look at me," Oodles said.

"Nor me." Wish-Wash looked up from his tea-pouring. 'Your daughter is hardly likely to confide in me. Did I tell you how she once said I looked like a cow. That reminds me though . . . "

He got up and headed for the door, and Oodles and James looked at each other.

Wish-Wash was carrying a parcel wrapped in brown paper when he returned, and skipped down the stairs beaming.

He passed it across the table. "Here you go, Jimbo. Happy birthday."

James took it and stared down. "For me? Really?"

"If it was for Wendy, don't you think I would have given it to her?"

"But . . . but . . . but I didn't get you anything, Bert. I'm embar-rassed now." His bottom lip quivered.

"Don't you worry, I'm used to being forgotten. The good thing is you'll know for next year. Go ahead and open it."

James started carefully peeling back the sticky tape.

"Rip it," Wish-Wash said. "Let yourself go for a change."

James did. He gulped as he uncoiled what was inside and draped it over his arm. It was a blue necktie with a naked lady set among palm trees.

"Like it?" Wish-Wash beamed. "I doubt you'll find another one like it. Don't blame me for the grease stains though. It was like that when I bought it."

TWENTY-FIVE
BIRTHDAY PRESENT DELIVERY

THEY WERE MUNCHING on toasted sandwiches for lunch when they heard the vehicle pull up.

Oodles got up from the table and went to his vantage point in the Venetian blinds. He cracked open a slat and looked out. "It's Moose and Awesome Sauce," he said. "They're removing a tarpaulin from the back of the ute."

Wish-Wash joined him at the window, opening a higher slat. "So it is. Do you reckon that's a jukebox they've got in the back?"

"Oh, for goodness sake." James dropped his cheese-and-ham toasty down on to his plate. "I hardly think Maddie would give me a jukebox for my birthday."

"Why not?" Wish-Wash said. "Remember the one they used to have in The Applecart? It used to have 100 versions in different languages of *Shaddup Your Face*."

"Steady, old mate," Oodles said. "It didn't have that many versions."

"Exaggerating again!" James said. "I only heard one version. One! But you're missing the point, Bert. No way would Maddie buy me a jukebox for my birthday. Especially one with that awful song on it."

"Maybe she had to compromise?" Wish-Wash said. "I'd imagine it's pretty hard to get jukeboxes with your beloved Beethoven on them."

"Oh, for goodness sake." James rose and headed for the door.

"Where are you going?" Wish-Wash said.

James stopped and turned. "I'm going outside to ask what it is. If it's a jukebox loaded with *Shaddup Your Faces*, I'll eat my hat."

Wish-Wash smirked. "You haven't got a hat. You'll have to swallow your mask instead. Don't forget it's on the top of the china cabinet?"

"Don't think I don't know what you've done, Bert? Very juvenile, as usual!" James had gone to the trouble of marking his mask with a marking pen, only to find identical marks on the other two. Goodness knows when this had been done? He could have been wearing the others' masks for weeks.

"Please yourself," Wish-Wash said. "But don't blame me if you die of COVID-19 on your birthday? That'll *Shaddup Your Face* for good. I wonder if someone in the Wind Tunnel Cafe got good odds on you carking it first?"

"Oh charming!" James turned towards the hallway, and slammed the door behind him.

TWENTY-SIX
TO WII OR NOT TO WEE

JAMES RETURNED 10 minutes later carrying a bottle of gin. "Quick, grab your toasties. We have to go out the back of the house. Moose and young Tim need to set up the TV equipment inside."

"TV?" Wish-Wash wiped his mouth with a hand. "I thought it was a jukebox?"

James put the gin bottle on the table and his hands on his hips. "What did I tell you, Bert? It was never going to be a jukebox. It's a widescreen TV AND a DVD player AND a Wii."

Wish-Wash made a gesture like he was squirting a fire hose into the air. "A wee?"

"Trust you to descend into toilet humour, Bert. Wii" — he spelt it out — "W. I. I . . . . Maddie thinks it's the answer to our exercise setbacks."

"Why doesn't she just get us Janey Fonda on DVD?"

"Because the Wii is much better than that outdated stuff. It comes with a disk called Wii Fit Plus, which that young American says has many activities we'll find fun."

Oodles smiled. "So you're letting Awesome Sauce come in the house this time?"

"As if I had a choice." James gestured towards the window. "I can hardly tell them to take the lot back to Maddie. Besides, she wouldn't have asked them to install it if she didn't think it was safe."

"Have you worked out who the kid is related to?"

James scratched his head. "Not really. Not at all, actually. Who?"

"Give it time. It'll probably come to you," Oodles said. "You're bound to see the resemblance."

"He seems to know what he's doing," James said. "He says he'll set everything up for us. All we'll need to do is hit the on-buttons and put in the disks."

Oodles picked up the gin bottle and inspected the label, "Why did they give you that?"

"That's a gift from my granddaughters," James said. "Maddie won't let Vicki and Velda see me, which is one of the few good things about my present circumstances. So they sent it in the ute with the other presents."

Oodles rotated the bottle and squinted at the label. "Bing Bong Mountain gin? I've never heard of it. But it must be from around here." He put the bottle down. "What made the girls buy it for you? I thought you only drank single-malt scotch?"

"I do." James scratched his stubble. "But what can you say? They're adopted. South Korea is a long way to send them back to."

"I've got a bottle of tonic water in the fridge." Oodles tapped the side of the bottle. "You should give G&Ts a go."

James raked his crew-cut with his fingers. "You must be joking. Quick, we need to go out the back door so these fellows can get inside and set everything up."

————

A blast of the horn told them Moose and Tim were leaving, which meant it was safe for them to go back into the house.

"See," James said proudly when they laid eyes on the widescreen TV. "It's the answer to our prayers!"

Oodles's face collapsed. "Both of the old TVs have gone!"

"Well, they had to make room for new stuff," James said. "I'm sure some scavenger will rescue them from landfill at the tip. One man's trash is another man's treasure, right?"

Oodles eyes nearly popped out. "I paid good money for that TV. I should have known better than to let Awesome Sauce into my house."

"Be fair to the kid. It's not like he didn't ask for permission to do it," James said.

Oodles fixed his angry eyes on Wish-Wash. "He never asked me, did he ask you?"

"Oh, for goodness sake," James said. "Neither of you were outside with me, were you? I gave him permission, OK!"

"You told him he could take my black and white TV to the tip? I don't think you realise the great sentimental value that old thing held for me? I saw Neil Armstrong take his great step for mankind on that telly."

"Get a grip, man," James said. "Everything has to die. Ask Neil Armstrong. But think what has just fallen into your lap? In a month, Bert and I will be gone but that TV and that DVD player and that Wii will still be there."

Oodles frowned. "You're not planning on taking them with you?"

"Why would I want the TV when the screen I've already got is twice as big. And there is nothing wrong with my blu-ray DVD player. Vicki has got them set up just the way I like it. Or maybe Velda has. I can't tell them apart. All Asians look the same to me."

Oodles frowned again. "Being identical twins has got nothing to do with it?"

"What do I get?" Wish-Wash blurted.

James turned. "What do you mean what do you get? Neither of those TVs belonged to you anyway."

The redness of Wish-Wash's face matched the colour of his trousers. "I'd argue I had a pretty strong emotional claim on the colour set because I watched the Janey Fonda video longer than either of you two blokes. The thing is I never told Awesome Sauce he could take it to the tip either. I'll skin him alive when I see him."

"Oh, go easy, you chaps. I can't tell you how lucky we are to have someone with that young lad's capabil—" James saw now the card-table had been relocated to another wall.

He groaned.

Even Hitler hadn't bombed Paris but his jigsaw looked like it had been strafed. The Arc de Triomphe was barely standing and the Eiffel Tower had disappeared. A small mountain of jigsaw pieces sat in a pile.

"Worked out where that Yank kid fits in yet?" Oodles asked. "Remember his grandfather? Tim Noah Junior?"

"You are kidding me!" A flashback movie started playing in James's head.

Awesome Sauce was the portly Texan billionaire's grandson?

The same Tim Noah Junior who had financially backed Moose in the 1990s in his quest to capture a Tasmanian Tiger?

The final straw came when he visited Windy Mountain and offered to buy the Northan apple orchard. James had flatly refused to sell but it turned out to be the worse business decision he had ever made, because that's when things really started to go downhill for him. His mental health, his political career, his marriage . . .

They heard a car pull up outside.

"Good. They're back," James said. "I'm going to give that idiot boy a piece of my mind."

Oodles was already looking out the blinds. "Bad luck then. It's not the museum ute. Dave Jenkins is getting out of his hearse."

"Dave Jenkins? Why would he visit us?" James gasped.

"Don't know," Oodles said. "He sure looks grim though."

"If he's carrying a scythe, it'll be for you for sure, Jimbo," Wish-Wash said.

"Oh, very funny, Bert."

"Well you said it. Everybody dies. It's probably your turn. I wish I had got my money on."

TWENTY-SEVEN
THE SUIT DIDN'T MAKE IT

THE UNDERTAKER HELD out a card when James opened the door.

James took it and studied it, but it made no sense. He frowned.

"My condolences," Dave Jenkins said.

"What for?"

"Your suit didn't make it."

"My suit?" James was puzzled, but then he remembered Dave's investment property, Taylor's Takeaway, had ventured into the dry-cleaning business. "Are you talking about my Italian suit made out of fine merino wool?"

"Forgive me if condolences is the wrong word. I'm breaking new ground here. But the point I'm trying to convey is the wool is not so fine now. Sorry. But we all make mistakes."

James' eyes widened. "This is unbelievable!"

"You were the one who sold the business to me in the first place. You said it was a real money-spinner."

"As a takeaway shop, you moron!"

"It's not my fault we had to cease normal operations during the lockdown. I have a moral responsibility to pivot so that I can keep the staff employed, and to help the community in a time of need."

"You've destroyed a perfectly good suit."

"Destroyed is a bit harsh. It's still good enough to accompany you on your final journey," Dave said.

"What?"

"If you have an open-casket viewing, no one will see the hole in the back of the jacket."

"What?" James's jaw was dropping further and further.

"That's what that voucher is for. We don't actually have any vouchers printed, which is why I had to improvise by scribbling it on a card. But please accept it as compensation for your loss. I'm sure you'll agree 30 per cent off for your funeral, when you need it, of course, represents great value."

James looked down at the card in his hand. It said the offer was valid for two years.

Dave read his mind. "The law requires us to limit it," he said quickly. "But don't worry, we've put your suit into cold storage and if I'm still around, I'll honour that voucher no matter how many years it takes."

James spoke slowly. "*If* you're still around?"

"You don't think funeral directors are immune from death, do you?"

"But what if you just sell the business? Will the new owner still honour the voucher?"

Dave blew a raspberry. "Who would buy this business in the state it's in? I thought COVID-19 would be a boon for us, but no one at all has died from it in this region and, worse, self-isolation has caused a drop in the fatality rate for the flu. And don't talk to me about social-distancing! When four pallbearers are needed to carry a casket, do you know how hard it is to stay the required distance apart? Downsizing the workforce to two to a coffin has doubled the rate of injury — bad backs, pulled muscles, assorted workers' compensation claims . . ."

TWENTY-EIGHT
THE OFFER STANDS

JAMES HAD BARELY CLOSED the door when knocking came from the other side.

He had expected to see Dave Jenkins still standing there.

Instead, when he opened the door, Conn Northan met his eyes. "You all right, cousin? Can't you find your razor?"

"What are you doing here?" James spluttered. "I didn't even see you walking up the hill."

"Dat's because I was crouching down on the other side of that big black car. Funny vehicle for a pizza delivery man."

"That was a hearse, you moron."

"Was it? You could have told me. I feel all icky now."

"Just don't tell Dave Jenkins you thought he was delivering pizza. It might give him ideas."

Conn studied his face. "You're not feeling all right, are you?"

"If you must know, my day started full of promise but it's deteriorating by the minute."

"Is dat right? Good ting I've brought some good news to cheer you up."

James forced himself to smile.

"Turns out you were right," Conn said. "About Messerschmitt's dog's name being Adolf?"

"Of course I was right. I'm just amazed you couldn't tell the difference between a male dog and a female dog."

"Dat's what worried me. But it became clear when Messerschmitt came home from the pound with Adolf who, it turns out, was doing a bit of remand time, too."

"He has *two* dogs now?"

"Aye. Two German Shepherds, Adolf and Eva. The good news is he's found a way to stop dem chewing your leather couches."

"My Chesterfields!"

"He's taken to locking dem in the dining room."

"The dining room? There's not room to swing a cat in there, never mind two great big dogs."

"Ah, dat's where you're wrong. It's surprising how much room you can make by decluttering."

"Decluttering?"

"A fella in a truck came and took away the table and chairs yesterday. I don't know why he had to remove dat nice picture of the hunt scene though."

"Not the oil painting! That cost a bomb." James's eyes nearly rolled into the back of his head. "So did the Queen Anne dining suite, come to think of it."

"Dat's why the man told Messerschmitt he'd get a good price for it, I suppose."

———

James returned to the living room in a daze. He now knew what it felt like to be thrown into the sea from a great height.

"You look like you've had some bad news, Jimbo?" Wish-Wash said.

"You can say that again."

"You look like you've had some bad news, Jimbo?"

"Oh, very twee. I've had two shocks in quick succession but I wouldn't expect you to understand."

"Try me."

A shrill whistle pierced the room.

Oodles walked to the window and peeled back a slat. "He's late. Gus is waiting at the gate waving a letter."

He turned to James at the same time Wish-Wash did. "It must be for you, Jimbo," they said in unison.

James headed back towards the door. "Oh, for goodness sake."

————

GUS FOOT handed the letter to James, who could see straight away it bore no stamp.

"It's from Messerschmitt again, Jimbo, isn't it?"

"You think?" James said.

"No need to be sarcastic. I'm just doing my job, you know. If it's in my mailbag, I deliver. Simple as that."

"Let me guess, you stopped at the public toilets again?"

Gus stared at him. "Are you trying to grow a beard?"

"Don't change the subject. Did or did you not have a toilet break?"

"It's always one crossword clue that stumps you."

"I knew it! Let me guess. When you came out you saw the man walking the dog on the far side of the oval again?"

Gus shook his head. "This time it was a man with two dogs."

"You don't think it might have been Messerschmitt?"

Gus gazed at the tree-tops again. "Hard to say. He was a long way away and walking away from me. But since when did Messy have two dogs?"

"Since a few days ago, I've been reliably informed." James flipped the envelope over. Once again, there was no return address.

"Aren't you going to open that?" Gus asked.

"I'm not sure I want to. He's been standing in the garden every night since the last time you were here. I can barely sleep knowing he's out there slapping that baseball bat into his hand."

"Opening that letter isn't likely to make it worse. Perhaps he wants to let you know he's calling a truce because you've withstood all the intimidation he's tried to force on you?"

"You don't know Messerschmitt?"

Gus stroked his beard. "Oh, I think I do. I've known lots of blokes just like him. Have you given any more thought to our little chat? Remember, for $10,000 I know blokes who can make Messy go away forever."

James ripped open the letter and examined the card inside.

Someone had scrawled *Happy Birthday, Uncle*. No name, no other marks.

"What did I tell you?" James turned the card around so Gus could see it. "It's clearly another threat."

Gus read it. "Interesting interpretation, Jimbo. But I wouldn't try to argue that in a court of law. Do yourself a favour, and just give me the word, and" — he clicked his fingers — "mineshaft here he comes."

TWENTY-NINE
THE GIN MIX-UP

WISH-WASH LOOKED up when James came inside from the letterbox.

His hands grasped three DVDs. "We have some gems here, Jimbo." Wish-Wash looked down again to inspect them further. "Hey, how come your daughter knew it was also my birthday when you didn't?"

James rubbed his prickly chin. "Is that where those came from?"

Wish-Wash waved the DVDs in James's direction. "I found them in a gift-wrapped parcel on top of the TV. The label said: Happy birthday, Bert."

"I'll be," James said. "That girl's got a better political compass than I gave her credit for. It is one thing knowing what colours you wear, it confounds me how she could possibly guess the type of dross you enjoy watching."

"Dross? What are you talking about?" Wish-Wash waved them more frantically. "These are flamin' cinematic classics."

"Will you be careful, Bert! You could take my eye out!"

"What do you want to watch first? *Bridge On The River Kwai*?" He started whistling the chorus of the Colonel Bogey March, then stopped. "*The Magnificent Seven*? Or *The Man Who Shot Liberty Valance*?"

"I'm not in the mood to watch any of your silly movies. What I need right now is a drink." James looked at Oodles. "Do you have any top shelf in the house, Clarence?"

Oodles shook his head and pointed to the bottle of gin on the table. "Only that, old son."

"What did you not understand when I intimated I would not be seen dead drinking that?"

"Oh, I don't think anyone apart from me and Wish-Wash is likely to see you, dead or otherwise." Oodles looked up at Wish-Wash. "Will you join us for a gin and tonic?"

"You must be flamin' joking!" Wish-Wash put the DVDs down on the china cabinet. "I haven't been strong all these years to blow it on gin, of all things."

"One little drink isn't going to hurt you, old son. Six parts water, one part gin. Lolly water really."

"Lolly water to you maybe! It's bound to go to my head after all these years. How would I be able to follow the movie then?" Wish-Wash started whistling the Colonel Bogey March again, with pretend hiccups this time.

"For goodness sake, you won't be watching *any* movies, Bert," James said.

Wish-Wash picked up the DVD on top of the pile and waved it in anger. "Who are you to tell me what I can and can't do with my birthday present?"

"You forget," James said. "You need *my* birthday present in order to play it — and right now, you don't have my permission because I need a stiff drink, and some peace and quiet."

Wish-Wash looked at Oodles, hoping for the support he usually got. But when Oodles just shrugged, he got the message.

"I hope you both choke on that grog." He stormed off to his bedroom.

———

Oodles poured the gin into the two long glasses. It came out in pale, glutinous globs.

He watched it slide slowly down the inside of the glasses with the consistency of treacle. "I've never seen gin like this."

"You sure it's even gin?" James took the bottle from him and sniffed into the opening. "It doesn't smell right to me."

"Maybe this is a new-fangled boutique gin?" Oodles said.

James rotated the bottle. "How come neither of us have even heard of this brand?"

"Beats me, old son. There couldn't be too many Bing Bong Mountains around though, so it's gotta be local."

"I don't like it," James said. "My ex used to drink gin, but it never smelt like this." He watched Oodles top up both glasses with soda water. "Nor did it have lazy bubbles like that."

Oodles picked up his glass and clinked the top of James's, which was still sitting on the table. "I'm too thirsty to care. Here's to your health, old cock. Happy birthday, once again."

The door bell rang.

Ding-dong, ding-dong.

———

Conn Northan was puffing when James opened the wooden front door.

"I ran back up the hill when I realised I had forgot to tell you something you'd probably want to know," the Irishman said.

James frowned. What could be so urgent?

"The carpet cleaners are booked in for next week." When James gave him a puzzled look, Conn continued, "They said they are going to give it their best shot."

"Their best shot?"

"Their best shot at getting out the green paint." Conn studied his face again. "You still look pale, cousin. Are you sure you're all right."

James straightened his hunched shoulders. "What you're telling me isn't making me feel any better."

"You've got to admire their bravery. It's their first time attempting to clean carpets."

James's voice rose. "They've never even done it before?"

"You can't blame Taylor's Takeaway for filling a community need when dis town happens to have no actual carpet-cleaning companies."

"Taylor's Takeaway!" James gasped. "Does Maddie know about this?"

"She's the one who booked dem. I wouldn't have done it myself, not after the ruckus with the hand-sanitiser."

"What ruckus?"

"Of course! You wouldn't have heard about dat? Taylor's Takeaway bought a gin still and converted it to make hand-sanitiser. When all dis is over, the plan is to switch back to making gin."

"Don't tell me? Bing Bong Mountain Gin?"

"So you have heard? Once again, you have to give dem full points for getting the gin labels printed up ahead of time. I wouldn't want to be dat employee who sent out the hand-sanitiser with the wrong labelling though. You don't want dead customers on your conscience, do you?"

"Oh, my goodness me!" James raked his closely-cropped hair. "Is it actually fatal if you drink it?"

"Dat's what the recall notice says," Conn said. "But from what I hear, you'd have to be pretty stupid to actually drink it. Hand-sanitiser looks and smells nothing like gin."

"But what if someone did drink it? Would they die?"

"I don't tink a small sip would harm you too much. But if you drank a whole glass you might know about it. Or maybe you wouldn't. Confusion is listed in the recall notice as one of the first symptoms. Dat's followed by vomiting, drowsiness, respiratory arrest, and finally death."

———

When James returned to the table inside, Oodles was wearing a silly grin.

His glass was empty.

James waved a shaking finger. "You drank that?"

Oodles smacked his lips together. "Told you I was thirsty."

"You drank it all!"

Oodles smiled. "I am just kidding you, old mate. I only had a sip. But it tasted so awful I poured it down the sink and drank the rest of the tonic water to wash away the taste."

"You know it was actually hand-sanitiser?"

Oodles searched James's eyes. "How do you know that?"

"Conn just told me. Taylor's Takeaway has gone into another side-line making gin and hand-sanitiser. It mixed up the labels."

THIRTY
WHAT WOULD WINNIE DO?

WISH-WASH DID NOT COME out of his bedroom for dinner that night. "I'm not hungry," came his sulking, muffled voice from the other side of the door.

When he got a whiff of the pizza though, he asked for his share to be slid through the crack underneath it.

"Don't be so bloody childish," Oodles shouted. "Even pizza won't fit under the door."

"It will if you remove the chunks of pineapple," Wish-Wash said.

"They don't put pineapple on seafood pizzas."

"Can't you at least slip me a prawn then?"

"No, if you want it, you'll have to come out and get it."

"I can't. I'm feeling sick. I don't want to infect anyone."

"Please yourself. We'll divide up your share between us. If you cark it overnight, Dave gave Jimbo a gift voucher giving him a discount for his funeral services. Let's hope it's transferrable."

———

As James chewed his pizza, he stole glances at Oodles masticating on the other side of the table.

He only had Oodles's word that he had only sipped the gin before tipping it down the sink. He could have actually drained it in one long gulp.

But the old man didn't seem to be succumbing to the symptoms Conn had mentioned. Confusion, drowsiness, respiratory arrest or vomiting. And certainly not death.

It paid to be ready though. The problem was James didn't even know how he was going to call the town ambulance because he had never seen a phone-book in the house.

He did know the phone number of the local general practitioner, Dr Jenkins. But it was only when he recalled the sequence that the irony hit him. Doc Jenkins was Dave Jenkins's father. It was bad enough when they had that doctor-undertaker link. But now Dave and Taylor's Takeaway had gone into the gin-poisoning business, more eyebrows might be raised.

And how would it look when people twigged James had sold Taylor's Takeaway to Dave in the first place? People might think he was getting a kickback, too! It would provide more grist for the Wind Tunnel Cafe rumour mill!

This is why he came to the decision he did. He didn't want to be there to witness Oodles's demise.

He put down his half-bitten slice of pizza, and sighed. "I'm going to have an early night, and read."

Oodles looked at his watch. "Strewth! It's not even 7 o'clock yet." He pointed to the rest of the pizza in the box. "You're not leaving me with all this?"

"Sorry, I couldn't stomach any more. It tastes like cardboard covered in tomato and cheese."

He had actually toyed with the idea of making the most of a Wish-Wash-free living room.

How nice would it be to not be pressured into having to play Scrabble.

He considered sitting in a corner and rebuilding Paris. But since he only had less than four more weeks left in captivity, he considered it very unlikely he could complete the 1000-piece jigsaw puzzle.

It was one thing leaving the TV, the DVD player and the Wii here, but he wasn't about to let Oodles put the last brick in the Arc de Triomphe. He'd never hear the end of it. And everyone who went into the Wind Tunnel Cafe would come out not just with indigestion but with a new piece of gossip.

"I want to be up early to check out the yoga program," he told Oodles.

"Yoga?"

"It makes sense now why Maddie was talking the Wii up the other day. We don't need to leave the living room to exercise now. It's all on the Wii."

"Don't bother waking me up. If you want to tie yourself in knots, old son, that's up to you."

———

When James looked out of his bedroom window, he knew he was in no danger of seeing Messerschmitt looking back at him.

Messerschmitt normally didn't appear at the edge of the garden until after 9pm, well after it was dark.

Why he'd stand where he did was anyone's guess? Even children knew not to stand under a gum tree. That umbrella wasn't going to protect his head if a big branch came tumbling down in the wind.

James drew comfort from the knowledge he would not have to drift off to sleep with the image burning into his brain of the man outside wearing the dark beanie and banging a baseball bat against his thigh.

James's light would already be out by the time Messerschmitt arrived.

James retreated from the window and sank back on to the bed.

He opened *Churchill: A Life*, by Martin Gilbert, on his e-reader. He had read it before, of course, but he really couldn't get enough of Winnie.

That old British bulldog would have never stood for the likes of Messerschmitt. Never mind falling branches, he'd have a B-17 Flying Fortress raining bombs down on his adversary's head.

THIRTY-ONE
A TASMANIAN TIGER
MOMENT

IT WAS FREEZING STANDING at the shaving mirror dressed only in his Y-fronts and singlet shortly before 6am. But James didn't have any other suitable attire for yoga.

He hadn't even intended to lather up. But when he brushed his chattering teeth, he had caught a reflection of himself and decided all that white stubble needed to go.

So here he was making slow, careful passes over his face.

He knew if he nicked himself, even just slightly, Maddie would find out and ask awkward questions.

Most likely she assumed he was still using the electric razor she had given him.

He hadn't accepted it graciously. "I've never cut myself badly. They wouldn't call it a safety razor if it wasn't safe."

"Oh, Daddy. It'd be just one less accident waiting to happen."

He had used the new electric razor once or twice but he was never happy with it.

So he went back to the method he had used as a teenager: razor blades and lather. What she didn't know, couldn't hurt her.

He splashed on some aftershave when he had finished, swished water around the sink to clean away his bits of discarded whiskers, and hurried to the relative warmth of the living room

Once he had closed the door to the hall, and shoved the last two logs from the metal woodbox into the stove in the kitchen, the space soon heated up.

Oodles and Wish-Wash never surfaced until around 8am, which gave him plenty of time to master the Wii yoga program.

The first task was easy. He had never had to stand on a balance board before but the deep breathing required was a cinch.

Things got a bit harder with the *Half-Moon* and the *Warrior* but it got really tricky when he had to do the *Tree*.

A phoney, mechanised voice emanating from the Wii told him that he was a little shaky.

"You'd be shaky, too, if you were on the verge of falling over," he shouted back loudly.

Really! He would have thought the *Tree* would be a tranquil pose. He could understand why you'd be asked to stretch your arms towards the sun and lock hands high above your head. But simultaneously standing on one leg was mad. Sliding your free foot up your one useful leg until it rested on your inner thigh was just asking for trouble.

James flicked the remote through the rest of the program.

Sun Salutation. No.

Standing Knee. No.

Palm Tree. He definitely was over trees.

Chair. Why, for heavens sake? There were already perfectly good chairs around the table.

Triangle. No. He had once played the Triangle in the orchestra at primary school. He still blamed his damaged hearing on the loudness of that percussion section.

He came to something he thought he could do.

That's how come he was down on all fours when Wish-Wash came bursting through the door.

"I heard shouting," he said. "Are you all right, Jimbo?"

James turned his head and groaned. "Do I look like I'm hurt?"

Wish-Wash continued looking down. "You know you have a hole in the back of your underpants? What is it you're trying to do?"

"If you must know, it's a yoga manoeuvre called *Downward-Facing Dog*."

Wish-Wash chortled. "You're not having another Tasmanian Tiger moment, are you?"

"For your information, the Wii is much too sophisticated to deal in extinct animals."

"You don't think that position is a bit easy?"

James rolled over, and checked his fitness tracker. His heart rate had edged up to 64 from his resting heart-rate of 63, but he wasn't about to tell Wish-Wash that. "It's a lot harder than it looks."

————

Conn had been right. Oodles didn't seem to be affected by his single sip of the hand-sanitiser.

If anything, he was more nimble than ever scrambling up the ladder and side-stepping on to the plank so he could paint up under the eaves.

It was about 11.30am. The weather was nice again and the old men were applying a second coat of green paint to the house.

James had just returned outside after his daily phone hookup with Maddie.

"It's about time you returned," Wish-Wash grumbled. "I'm bursting to go."

James gave him a searing glare. "I was only on the phone, not in the lavatory."

Wish-Wash pointed upwards. "Someone had to stay here in case Oodles fell off his perch."

James looked up at Oodles. "It's never worried you before."

"Yes, Wish-Wash," the man working above agreed. "I told you: go. I haven't fallen off a plank yet. But worse-case scenario, if I did take a tumble, I'd still be writhing on the ground when you came back out."

Wish-Wash stooped down and put his brush into the turps container, then removed his Matisse smock to reveal his blue singlet and his lurid track pants. "You blokes need to take health and safety more flamin' seriously," he grumbled.

He waved his finger at James. "You just keep an eye on the old bloke up there. Oodles is not as young as he used to be."

THIRTY-TWO
KUNG FU FIGHTING

TWENTY-FIVE MINUTES HAD PASSED and Wish-Wash still hadn't returned.

"Do you think he's fallen in?" James asked.

Oodles jumped down. "I wouldn't worry, old son. He's probably just got the trots."

As he was bending down to clean his brush in the turps a smashing sound came from inside, followed by a pained cry.

They rushed inside where they discovered Wish-Wash lying face-down on the floor sobbing and kicking his feet and banging his fists.

"What's wrong?" Oodles gasped.

Wish-Wash lifted his head towards the TV screen. "Look!"

That's when they saw it.

The TV was still working, with the same mechanised voice James had heard earlier, but now there was a crack that stretched like forked lightning from the top left of the screen to the bottom right, and the remote control lay on the floor.

"My birthday present!" James screeched.

Wish-Wash sat up and used his knuckles to wipe both eyes dry. "I didn't think you'd mind if I had a go."

"You were supposed to be outside painting, not doing yoga."

"I wasn't doing the flamin' yoga. I thought the kung fu workout would be more my pace."

"Kung fu? You?"

Wish-Wash wiped away his tears again.

James looked up to the ceiling.

"It's not my fault I don't know my own strength," Wish-Wash blubbered. "The program voice said for me to hold the remote in my right hand and the nunchuks in my left. Good thing I couldn't find them, eh? They could have done some real damage."

"You cretin." James waved his hand at the cracked TV. "What do you think this is?"

"Why are you going off at me?" Wish-Wash pointed to the screen. "The little voice deserves at least part of the blame. When he said kick, I kicked. When he said to punch with my right hand, I gave it all I've got. He could have flamin' reminded me I was still holding the remote in that hand and it was likely to fly out."

———

"You have ruined it for us all now," James said. "That TV would have helped us through our last month locked up here."

"Jimbo has a point, old son," Oodles said. "It's not just the next month I'm worried about either. He was going to leave everything here for me."

"It's still working, see," Wish-Wash said. Just then the phoney voice told him to breathe deeply. "When you burst in, I thought you blokes were concerned for me. Turns out, you're more worried about the flamin' telly."

James put his hands on his hips. "We can't watch it like that. That crack would give me a headache for sure."

"I dunno. It's not so bad," Wish-Wash said. "Nothing a bit of sticky-tape wouldn't cover up."

James heaved a big sigh. "You're joking! You'd have to chose between watching *The Bridge on the River Crack* or *The Man Who Shot Sticky-tape Valance.*"

"I think you're making a mountain out of a mole-hill," Wish-Wash said. "The last TV in that spot hadn't worked at all since 1969. At least this one is still operating."

"I'm afraid I agree with Jimbo this time, old son," Oodles said. "A month watching that will be hard enough, but it's got to last me for the rest of my life."

Wish-Wash put his arm out and Oodles helped him up.

"You could always think laterally," Wish-Wash said. "I bet there are a lot of pilgrims who would pay good money to see the religious image that has mysteriously appeared on your TV screen."

James stabbed a finger towards the crack. "I've never heard of the holy spider. Not in the C of E anyway." He looked at Oodles. "What about you Micks?"

Oodles shook his head.

"You haven't heard of the Virgin Mary, Jimbo?" Wish-Wash said.

"The Virgin Mary? I see no resemblance."

"That's because you are looking at this all wrong." Wish-Wash made the Sign of the Cross, though it might have been a gesture he had seen traffic cops do. "If you looked closely, that's the spitting image of the Virgin Mary's crack."

———

The doorbell rang.

Ding-dong, ding-dong.

"That'll be for you, Jimbo," Oodles and Wish-Wash cried in unison.

James surveyed the cracked TV again. "You sure about that? Perhaps the devil is on a recruitment drive."

Oodles looked sideways at him. "I thought you lot didn't believe in hell?"

"I'm willing to make an exception if he wants to take Bert away."

THIRTY-THREE
DYING IN A DITCH

THE MAN he opened the door to did not have horns and a pitchfork.

But his face was very red.

"He's gone," Conn Northan blurted.

"Who's gone?"

"Your nephew."

James forgot his TV woes for an instant, and slapped his thigh. "Really? Messerschmitt has moved out? That's great news!"

"Not really. It means I have to feed his dogs."

James's grin turned into a frown. "He didn't take Adolf and Eva with him?"

"No, the dogs are still at home chewing up the Chesterfields."

James gasped. He cherished that leather lounge suite. "I thought they were locked in the dining room?"

"I had to let dem out. They had nothing to eat in dat room."

"So, where's Messerschmitt gone?"

Conn shook his head. "He didn't tell me. He just didn't come home last night. I was hoping you had seen him?"

James snarled: "I see him every night." He stabbed his thumb back over his shoulder. "He stands in the garden with a baseball bat. It's his way of intimidating me."

"So you saw him last night? Dat reassures me he's all right."

It was now James remembered he hadn't actually seen the villain. He had only assumed he was on the other side of the window. "Why wouldn't he be all right?" he said slowly.

"I'd hate to think someting has happened to him."

———

James didn't bother going back inside. When Conn walked back down the hill, James took up a watching post by the letterbox.

What had Gus Foot done?

James looked at his watch. Gus was late again. No one else he knew had such difficulty with *The Pick of the Crop* crosswords.

Every now and then a noise in the window told him Wish-Wash or Oodles had cricked back a slat to snoop out, wondering what was going on.

Let them wonder. James wasn't about to validate their sticky-beaking by turning around and waving.

Finally, the sound of a motorbike told James Gus was working his way up the hill. It enraged James every time the engine cut out. Was everyone in the damn cul-de-sac getting a letter?

Gus's helmet appeared over the brow of the hill, and the rest of him followed.

James flagged him as if he were hailing a bus.

Gus handed him a flyer. "Patience, Jimbo. I was going to drop one in your box anyway. Everyone is getting one."

James looked down at the glossy paper fluttering in his hands. It was from Taylor's Takeaway, advertising their new carpet-cleaning sideline.

"They've got a cheek, if you ask me," Gus said when he saw the look on James's face. "Have you heard about their gin fiasco? They ought to be spending their advertising money on alerting more people about that if you ask me."

"Never mind that," James said. "Did you hear that Messerschmitt has disappeared?"

"No," Gus looked puzzled. "You sure?"

"My so-called cousin says he didn't come home last night."

"You don't think he drank the poison gin, do you?"

"How do I know? But I want to make sure it has nothing to do with you."

"Me?"

"You're the one who offered to hire those hitmen on my behalf."

"But you never agreed to it. I never got further than preliminary discussions with them."

"Preliminary discussions!" James's voice hit a crescendo. "Goodness gracious, you didn't mention my name, did you? What if they got mixed up and thought you were giving them the go-ahead?"

"Relax, Jimbo. These guys are professionals. They don't fuck up. It's much more likely Messy really did drink the gin. But I've known blokes like him most of my life. A bad batch of hooch won't kill him. Mark my word, he's probably sleeping it off in some ditch as we speak."

THIRTY-FOUR
MISSING

HE USED to lie awake wondering if he was on the verge of another heart attack when he knew Messerschmitt was outside his bedroom window.

But James had a new problem.

Six nights had gone by since he had last seen the thug standing in the garden.

Now he lay awake wondering where Messerschmitt was, and listening to his heartbeats in case he skipped some.

He wished he had taken greater heed of advice he had read some-where about what to do if you suffered a heart attack while alone. It took you through some kind of do-it-yourself CPR that involved coughing, but James had only skimmed through the first half of the article before dismissing it as bunkum.

No wonder he was looking hagged! He had only strung together a few fitful hours of sleep in nearly a week, and he had given up on shaving once again.

"You're starting to look like the Wild Man of Borneo gone to seed," Oodles taunted him over breakfast.

The smell of burned toast assaulted James's nostrils, and the radio was crackling some awful country music as the three of them sat around the yellow table.

"Give me a break," James said, looking sideways. "Bert here has made that look all his own."

"Hmm," Wish-Wash said. "At least I'm not auditioning to be the new Kenny Rogers. The poor bloke has only been dead for a few weeks."

James looked vacantly at him. "Did I know him?"

"I doubt it. You obviously didn't know *of* him." He pointed towards the kitchen where the radio noise was coming from. "You must have heard about his death on the news? American country music singer with a silver beard just like the one you're trying to grow?" He broke into a song with a faux croaky voice, something about playing poker.

"Will you stop that," James cried. "I think I'd rather go listen to the toilet being flushed than listen to that noise. Bad enough I have to put up with that radio all day, now I've got to listen to a hairy ape singing very badly."

Wish-Wash stopped. "That's charming, that is." He looked at Oodles. "Don't you think so, cobber? Who's he to call *me* a hairy ape?"

James rubbed his chin. "Anyway, at least I have an excuse for not shaving. It's not your nephew who's missing!"

Wish-Wash cried: "That's not fair. I shave!"

"When?" James said.

"I forgot to bring my razor into lockdown, that's all."

"You have a razor?"

"'Course I do." Wish-Wash smiled. "Slutz Plains Op Shop had a cut-price cut-throat sale."

"Unbelievable! Even your razor is second-hand?" James said. "I'd never use a blade if I didn't know where it had been. It could carry hepatitis. Or have been used as a murder weapon."

Oodles and Wish-Wash both looked at him.

James hadn't told Oodles and Wish-Wash how Gus Foot had offered to hire hitmen on his behalf to get rid of Messerschmitt, but he had shared with them the postman's theory that Messerschmitt was probably sleeping off the effects of gin/hand-sanitiser. Well, he had to tell them something! Wish-Wash had the same view from his bedroom window, so they would both have known the thug wasn't turning up each night.

But six nights lying in a ditch? That was some serious kind of hangover.

"Why don't you flag down Gus, see if he's heard anything?" Oodles said.

"Yeah," Wish-Wash agreed. "Gus keeps his ear to the ground."

"Certainly not!" James threw out a hand like a stop signal. "I wouldn't even contemplate delaying the progress of the Queen's mail."

He wasn't about to tell them he feared Gus might confess he had accidentally activated the hitmen.

"The Queen's mail?" Oodles scratched his head. "How long has it been since you posted a letter, old son? The last stamp I bought had Richie Benaud's face on it, not the Queen's"

James clicked his tongue. "The whole mail service has gone downhill, if you ask me. Postmen used to ride bicycles and politely blow a whistle. Now we have dead cricketers gracing stamps and the Leader of the Mail Pack who wolf-whistles when he's just dropped a letter into your letterbox."

James waved a trembling finger towards the kitchen. "Is it too much to ask we had a decent radio that informed us what was happening in the world?"

"There's nothing wrong with that wireless out in the kitchen," Oodles said. "It hasn't missed a beat since we got it as a wedding present."

"Don't you think it's time it was retired!"

"What for? They made things to last in those days. It might even be older. I suspected at the time it was actually second-hand." Oodles glanced at Wish-Wash. "Who gives hand-me-downs as wedding gifts?"

"I didn't even know you then, cobber, so don't look at me." Wish-Wash dropped his voice. "Mind you, if I ever were invited to a wedding, the Slutz Plains Op Shop would be a great place to find a present."

Wish-Wash made eye contact with James. "That reminds me, how was that bottle of Greek wine we gave you?"

"Wine? You jest! I'm not sure you can even call Raki wine. But good heavens, you're not telling me the concoction that passes for drain-cleaner is second-hand, too."

"Oppy used to think it tasted like nectar of the gods."

"Who?"

"You know? The Greek bloke who ran the fish'n'chip shop in Slutz Plains until he dropped dead over the cooker and deep-fried his hands and his head."

James dropped his toast on to his plate. "Did you have to tell me that when I'm eating? Remind me never to buy a takeaway from that shop."

"I'm pretty sure they've changed the fat." Wish-Wash flashed his rotten teeth. "I just thought you'd want to know about that bottle of Raki we gave you. It's got predominance."

James's eyes narrowed. "It's got what?"

"You know? The history of the ownership."

"I think the word you're looking for is *provenance*." James unfurled an outstretched palm. "But please don't tell this … this … Greek in batter once owned that bottle?"

"He was a Cretan."

"Yes, that would explain why he thought it tasted like nectar then."

"No, I mean he came from Crete. I'm not even sure what his name even was. Cratis Something-Opolous. We just called him Oppy. He'd roll in his grave if he knew his widow cleared out all his belongings before he was even cold, which now I think about it, probably took some time."

James picked up his abandoned toast and dropped it on to Wish-Wash's plate.

"Really? You don't want it?"

"No, I've lost my appetite."

Wish-Wash picked it up and examined it. "You sure you didn't lick it? There's not much honey on it."

James pushed the honey jar towards Wish-Wash. "Feel free to have some more."

Wish-Wash continued his story as he layered more honey on. "Maria dropped all Oppy's clothes, his pipe, his ashtrays and three boxes of Raki at the Op Shop charity bin. So you're the lucky beneficiary of two of those items."

"Two? You only gave me one bottle?"

"I also gave you the tie he was wearing when he died. With the naked lady, remember?"

James buried his head in his hands. "That's another thing I didn't need to know." He looked up. "How did we get on to this anyway?"

"You don't like my wireless," Oodles said.

"Nonsense," James said. "I'm sure Bakerlite will come back into fashion one day. I just wish it wasn't stuck on the same channel?"

"What have you got against country music?" Oodles said.

"Apart from the fact it's all in the key of American twang, you mean, and that station doesn't even have a decent news service?"

"What are you talking about?" Oodles said. "It has news on the hour."

"Oh yes, you can find out everything you need to know about the revolving door of marriages in tinseltown, and the Lotto numbers. I'm talking about real news, things that affect people."

"You want to hear how many people are dying around the world? How depressing!"

"If indeed they are dying. How would we ever know? And how about some local news?" James put on his news-reader's voice. "*A man wearing a beanie, brandishing a baseball bat and clutching a half-consumed bottle of hand-sanitiser is recovering in hospital after falling into a ditch and breaking his leg."*

"You wish," Wish-Wash said. "But perhaps it is time for Awesome Sauce to have a look at that radio to try to move it on to another station. I have to phone him about something else. I could ask him?"

James's eyes darted sideways. "Don't you dare!"

THIRTY-FIVE
STRETCH

THE DOORBELL RANG.

Ding-dong, ding-dong.

"That'll be for you, Jimbo." Oodles and Wish-Wash said in unison.

"At this time of the morning?" James looked around at the stained living-room door.

"Perhaps they've let the Jehovah's Witnesses out again," Wish-Wash said. "Better put on your mask in case their religious zeal is contagious."

James heaved a sigh as he pulled himself up from his chair. Wish-Wash knew fine well he had given up wearing his mask because he was the clown who had started marking everyone's mask the same way so nobody knew which was which.

James walked past the three masks that sat on the top of the china cabinet next to the tangle of fitness-trackers. James had finally thrown his black wrist-band on the pile, too. In truth, he was just as fed up as the others about the incessant vibrations. But he didn't tell Oodles and Wish-Wash that. Instead, he had blamed his exasperation on Wish-Wash because, he claimed, by cracking the TV screen the clumsy oaf had put an end to the exercise that might just have prolonged his life.

James opened the door into the hallway.

What did Conn want this time?

He opened the front door and came face to face with a tall man with a blue uniform and cap.

"Sergeant Stretch!"

"Mr Northan." You look like you were expecting someone else?"

James felt the blood drain from his face. "I should have known you'd want to interview me."

"You did? I came here to speak to Oodles but . . . " He eyed James's sunken, bewhiskered face. "Are you all right?"

"Not really. You'll want to know what I know about Messer-schmitt's disappearance?"

Stretch looked him in the eye. "I didn't even know he was missing."

"I had just assumed he was supposed to check into the police station regularly under the terms of his bail?"

Stretch adjusted his cap and whistled out a stream of minty breath. "Now you mention it, I haven't seen him at the station for days. I'll have my constables' guts for garters. They're supposed to be keeping tabs on him." He pinched his mono-eyebrow. "Mind you, we've been up to our eyeballs in distractions lately. Did you hear about the gin substitution cock-up? Tracking down the last bottle is proving very difficult."

"Really? I think I can help you with that."

"You can?"

James pointed down the hall. "The empty bottle is at the back door. I'll fetch it for you."

Stretch's eyes widened. "You drank it? No wonder you don't look well."

"No. Clarence poured it down the sink."

"He did?"

"You wanted to speak to him?" James turned sideways and yelled. "Clarence! Someone for you."

James heard a groan, followed by the creak of a chair.

"Are you sure it's for me?" Oodles said, as he came through from the living room. Then he turned the corner and saw the policeman. "Stretch! What brings you here?"

Stretch grimaced. "I don't believe them for a moment, Oodles, but an allegation has been made. You understand I'm duty-bound to question you?"

Oodles looked at him blankly. "Question me about what?"

James started to turn. "Um, I'll just go fetch that bottle."

Oodles caught him by the shoulder and turned him back. "Do I need a witness?"

"I don't think so," Stretch said. "I'm pretty sure this is just a scurrilous claim, and your denial will be good enough for me to file the paperwork."

"What kind of scurrilous claim, old son?"

Stretch cleared his throat. "You sure you want Mr Northan to hear this? With his connections?"

"Don't be so bloody silly. We have no secrets in this house." He glanced at James. "Do we, old mate?"

"Up to you, Oodles." Stretch reached up and caressed the green weatherboards above the door. "I see you've been painting?"

"We've still got some bibs and bobs to do around the garden, but we finished painting the house yesterday. Like it?"

"Well, the thing is . . ." Stretch said. " . . . we've had an allegation you've used stolen paint."

Oodles straightened up and spluttered. "Who's telling you that bulldust?"

"I'm not at liberty to reveal who. What I do need is a response from you."

"You don't believe them, do you?"

Stretch pulled out his notebook from his pocket and started to write. "I'll take that as a denial."

"You can check the empty tins if you like." Oodles's voice became tremulous. "They're around the back. I've got a bunch more of them unused in the garage. I've even got a receipt for them somewhere."

James knew this was bluff. Oodles couldn't possibly have a receipt. What's more, the tins all carried labels that declared them the property of the Windy Mountain Council.

James turned. "I'll just go get that gin bottle."

As he left, he heard Stretch say Oodles's word was good enough for him.

Well! He would say that wouldn't he? When Stretch first came to Windy Mountain as a young junior constable whose face was covered in bum fluff and pimples, Oodles and Madge had taken him in as a boarder. He might have even slept in the bedroom James was in now, probably before it had that mouldy smell. Stretch was well into middle-age now but that bond remained.

When James returned with the bottle, Oodles and Stretch were chatting amicably.

"Oodles was just telling me about how you came into possession of the fake gin, Mr Northan. Your granddaughters would have been mortified if it had killed you."

"I doubt it. They're probably anxious to see what I've left them in my will." James handed the empty bottle over. "I hope though this gives you the evidence to throw the book at Taylor's Takeaway."

"Thanks. Hopefully, the people at the police lab can find what they need." Stretch stooped down and put the bottle on the ground, and poised his pen above his notebook. "What can you tell me about Messerschmitt, Mr Northan?"

"Only that he's been missing for nearly a week now."

Stretch started writing. When he had finished, he said: "And how do you know this?"

"Good heavens, he's my nephew, isn't he? What's more, he's staying at my place."

Stretch bent his knees and looked over James's shoulder into the house. "Here?"

"No, not here. In my cottage with that thick-as-a-brick Irishman who's pretending to be my cousin."

"Who?" Stretch searched his face for a clue.

"Oh, for goodness sake. Don't you know about anything happening in this town, sergeant? Conn Northan!"

THIRTY-SIX
SECRET HIDING PLACE

THE OLD MEN each peeled back a slat in the blinds and watched the police car disappear down the hill.

"Why didn't you tell him Messerschmitt had been standing in the garden each night, old son?" Oodles asked.

"It hardly seems relevant," James said.

"Hardly relevant? I'd reckon it's crucial information."

"I wouldn't have told him anything if he hadn't ambushed me. Remind me not to answer the door when it's for someone else!"

Oodles was smiling as he sat back down at the table. "I think I did a pretty good job getting him off my back."

"You've got that policeman wrapped around your little finger! What if he had accepted your invitation to look in the garage?"

Oodles knocked on his head with a knuckle. "*Oh, I've forgotten where I put the key. You'll have to come back, Stretch.*"

"Whoa," Wish-Wash said. "What did Stretch want?"

"Some rat has accused me of stealing the paint we used to do the house."

"But you did!" James said.

Oodles clicked his tongue. "They'll have a hard time proving it. It'll be their word against an old man who served the council loyally for all those years."

Oodles studied James's face for a moment. "Hey, you're not the joker who dobbed me in, are you?"

"When have I had the chance? But just don't expect me to start perjuring myself by lying for you"

"OK, but just remember this." Oodles waggled a finger. "If I go down, we'll be taking you down with me." He glanced at Wish-Wash. "Isn't that right, old son?"

Wish-Wash folded his arms. "Just leave me out of it."

"What?" Oodles's mouth fell open.

Wish-Wash thrust out his bottom lip. "I didn't get much support from you when I had the accident with the TV. Seems to me the boot is on the other foot now."

Wish-Wash looked like he was wounded. Then he turned his venom on to James. "You know how to hurt a bloke's feelings, too. You haven't worn that tie I gave you for your birthday even once."

He banged a fist on the tabletop. "I've had a gutful of the both of you."

———

Oodles and James had a good view of Wish-Wash painting the garden bench on his own.

They were further down the garden, painting the bird-bath together.

Oodles leaned over and whispered. "It doesn't seem right. I always meant us to paint that bench together. It's our meeting place."

James scoffed. "We've only sat on that particular bench three times."

Oodles dipped his brush in the paint tin, wiped it on the rim, and watched the excess green paint dribble back down the inside. "But it's symbolic, isn't it?"

"It's a foot short for three grown men, that's what it is."

"I get that. But what I mean is the three of us spent a lot of time sitting on the bench in the High Street. Now we can't go there, that short-arsed bench over there is all we've got. We should be doing it together."

"You heard Bert. If he really thinks the two of us are getting on his nerves, he's better off working on his own anyway."

"I don't get it, old son. Wish-Wash and I haven't always seen eye-to-eye but he's never pushed me away like this. It's different with you. He's only ever really tolerated you at best."

Oodles resumed slapping on the paint around the base. "You don't think Wish-Wash was the one who dobbed on me?"

"Bert? Why would he do that? How, even?"

"We don't know who he speaks to on the phone? Maybe he's shopped me to the Crimestoppers' hotline?"

"Would he do that?"

Oodles shrugged. "I wish now I had been more conciliatory when he smashed that TV."

"You had every right to be angry. I know I was. For him to say today he's hurt I haven't worn his tie smacks of diversionary tactics." James pinched at his overalls. "A tie with these? Pleeeaaase!"

"I've been thinking." Oodles pinched the bridge of his nose with his left hand. "Perhaps we should move all that paint out of the garage? Without Wish-Wash knowing."

"Really? When?"

"Tonight. You and me."

"Both of us!" James's voice ascended from a whisper to a cry.

"Shush." Oodles placed a finger on his lips. "It would take too long on my own. Besides, you're up to your neck in this. You'd be helping to cover your own tracks, too."

James sighed. "Where are we going to put it?"

Oodles nodded in Wish-Wash's direction. "See that little door behind him that leads to under the house. We could stack all the tins of paint in there. That way, if someone raids the garage they won't find anything."

"I thought you said you weren't worried about Sergeant Stretch?"

"I'm not. But if I'm right and Wish-Wash did dob me into Crimestoppers, the higher-ups might overrule young Stretch and send in a SWAT team."

———

The subject of food helped Wish-Wash forget he wasn't actually talking to the others. He even fetched the dish of food that had been left on the front mat.

"Is this what I think it is?" he asked as he placed the warm dish on the table.

Oodles and James looked at each other. Wish-Wash knew fine well Katy had cooked a steak'n'kidney pie because she had asked him on the phone if everyone liked kidneys.

James could never understand why someone would want to ruin a perfectly good steak pie by adding kidneys to it, but he didn't get a say in the matter.

"Of course we all like kidneys," Wish-Wash had blurted into the mouthpiece. "Is the Pope a Catholic?"

When he hung up, James wanted to know what had transpired in the conversation

"I was putting in our dinner order," Wish-Wash said. "Someone's got to organise the tucker."

"But did I hear you say I like kidneys?"

"So? I made an executive decision."

"Did you? Good thing I'm not allergic to them then."

"I knew that."

James looked him in the eye. "You did, did you? How? Did Nostradamus predict it?"

"Who?"

"Never mind. Just thank your lucky stars I don't hate them. Too late now, but I don't care for them either."

Wish-Wash approached the dinner like a treasure hunt. The person who found the most kidneys won.

When James pointed out it wasn't a contest, Wish-Wash charged on regardless. He said the winner ought to be allowed to pick the movie they watched that night. He'd be going for *The Magnificent Seven*.

Oodles said Wish-Wash could please himself what he watched because he and Jimbo planned to resume tracking their steps around the outside of the house again.

Wish-Wash started choking on a mouthful of gravy and possibly a kidney that had gone down the wrong way.

When he recovered from his coughing fit, he warned them not to expect him to come to the rescue if one of them tripped over a paint tin in the dark outside.

Oodles told him he didn't need to worry because they had cleaned up this time.

Wish-Wash wiped his mouth with a hand. So they'd be trotting out the fitness trackers again?

No, Oodles said. This time they were going to count their steps the old-fashioned way.

———

Oodles started passing the tins through the little door.

James felt like a commando shuffling around on his tummy and reaching out to discover storage space and hopefully not a spider.

Only when he turned around did he see the weak stream of light that came over Oodles's shoulders.

Oodles hadn't wanted to turn the outside lights on. He didn't want to draw attention to what they were doing.

So the only illumination came from street lights and the moon, which flickered in and out of the clouds.

This proved to be adequate when they were gathering up the empty tins from around the back and transferring the full cans from the garage, stacking them near the little door in readiness for their new home.

But under here it was pitch black when you faced inwards. You really needed a flashlight. James knew there was one sitting on the mantlepiece in the kitchen. But Oodles didn't want to go inside and get it because he said it would just make Wish-Wash suspicious.

"Mind your head, old son," Oodles whispered.

"Will you stop saying that! You know I've already bumped my head twice."

"That's why you need to be careful. I don't want you damaging the floorboards."

"Oh, very funny." James grabbed another tin by the ring, which cut into his fingers.

"I thought I'd be able to hear Bert's video blaring from under here," James whispered.

Oodles poked his head inside and listened. "You're right. I can't hear anything either. I'd reckon that's a good thing though. If we can't hear him, he can't hear us."

THIRTY-SEVEN
IN THE PINK

WISH-WASH WAS NO where to be seen when they returned inside an hour later.

The TV was off, too.

The dinner dishes remained dirty on the sink. James guessed the one that looked like it had been licked clean belonged to Wish-Wash and it really had been licked clean.

"He must have gone to bed early," Oodles said.

"He could have washed the dishes for a change."

Oodles shook his head. "Did you ever visit him when he lived above the museum?"

"Why on earth would I have visited him?"

"If you had you'd know he only ever washes up when he comes to the end of a dinner set."

"You let him get away with murder, Clarence. It's your house. You're within your rights to put your foot down."

Oodles scratched his chin. "What would you have me do? Drag him out of his bedroom kicking and screaming?"

"Why not? Someone needs to teach him some respect!"

———

James screamed as soon as he walked into the bathroom.

"Good grief! Come see what he's done, Clarence."

When Oodles came in, he was carrying a clean pair of overalls. "I thought you'd be wanting these in the morning. You're covered in spider webs."

Then he saw what James was seeing.

The sink was matted with bits of Wish-Wash's grey whiskers.

"I don't believe it," James screeched. "No wonder he's already gone to bed. He's only gone and shaved off his beard. He's probably discovered three double chins he didn't know he had, and is embarrassed."

"Are we talking about the same bloke, old son?" Oodles said. "I've never actually seen Wish-Wash embarrassed. Angry, yes. But not embarrassed."

"This might be a first then. *The Magnificent Seven* might have gone to his head. He might have gone all Yul Brynner on us."

Oodles kept staring at the mess in the sink. "What? You reckon he's shaved his head, too?"

"Hard to say. This all looks like his whiskers hair to me. No telling though what he's actually washed down the sink."

Oodles shook his head. "That's all I need? A sink clogged up with hair!"

Then he noticed what was sitting on the bench. "My good scissors! He didn't even put them back in the drawer!"

———

The top of Wish-Wash's head was wrapped in a towel when he wafted through the living-room door for breakfast the next morning.

James and Oodles had already eaten their cereal and were munching pieces of toast and marmalade.

"You are alive, babyface," Oodles put down his toast and turned his head. "Jimbo and I were just discussing who gets what of your belongings. You can keep that pong you have on you though." He sniffed the air. "What is it? Aftershave?"

Wish-Wash surveyed the room, then sighed. "There is no where else to sit. Guess that means I'm stuck with you two bozos."

He sat down at the yellow table and studied the cluster of jars and cereal packets. "Is that marmalade?"

"You know it is. Katy made it," Oodles said. "But don't try to distract us. Not only did you use my good scissors, you left a helluva mess in the sink, which is still there waiting for you to clean up, by the way."

"Don't get your knickers in a knot. I'm going to clean it up, I just got thrown a bit last night. I had a nasty shock when I did my head in the bath."

Oodles and James looked at each other. They hadn't thought to look for hair in the bath.

Wish-Wash looked at James. "Sorry about the clogged twin-blades. I hope you have a new cartridge for when you start shaving again?"

"What?" James spluttered. "You used my razor?"

"I hope you don't mind. I had to use your bottle of aftershave, too.
"

"My expensive French aftershave? All of it?"

"It was a major shave." Wish-Wash held his glare. "But fair's fair. I used Oodles's scissors to cut the whiskers down to a shaveable length. I wasn't about to use his razor, too. And he didn't have much Brut left in his bottle."

Oodles and James glanced at each other again and Wish-Wash picked up on the body language.

"Big deal!" Wish-Wash said. "You weren't even using your razor, Jimbo. It's not like I used it to shave my pubes."

"Two out of three still is still not good," James said. "Your face, your head . . . "

Wish-Wash scowled. "My head? You think I shaved my head?"

"Why else are you wearing that towel?"

"Yeah, well." Wish-Wash pointed to his head covering. "You can blame Awesome Sauce for this?"

"Awesome Sauce?" Oodles said. "What's he got to do with the price of blinking eggs?"

Wish-Wash sighed heavily. "When I asked him to buy me some hair dye, I assumed he'd know I wanted black."

He removed his towel to reveal his new pink coiffure. "Christ Almighty, I sure hope this grows out in our last three weeks here before anyone else sees me. My bet is it'll be a race to see which comes out first." He waved a hand over his hair. "This? Or the pink staining in the bath?"

THIRTY-EIGHT
LONG ARM OF THE LAW

THE DOORBELL RANG.

Ding-dong, ding-dong.

"Oh, I'm getting a bit tired of this?" James dabbed marmalade from his mouth with his serviette and got up. "Who do you think it is this time?"

"If it's Awesome Sauce, tell him I have a bone to pick with him," Wish-Wash said.

James swung around and stood up, placing his hands on his hips. "What makes you think it might be that idiot boy, pray?"

"Easy. I asked him to drop by. What else are you going to do with the flamin' radio? Fix it yourself?"

James rolled his eyes. "I'll ask Maddie to buy me a tranny."

Oodles looked at him hard. "I don't think they still make transistors, old son. If you ask for a tranny nowadays, you might get something you didn't actually bargain for."

James huffed, and turned for the door.

———

As soon as he opened up and saw the blue uniform, James broke into a sweat.

"Sergeant Stretch! It's you again?"

The policeman produced a notebook from his pocket. "Sorry, sir. New information about your nephew's disappearance has come to light, and I need to ask some follow-up questions."

James blinked slowly. "But I've told you everything I know."

"You didn't tell me he's been standing in your garden each night trying to intimidate you. I knew there had to be a reason you were looking so rough. He was trying to put the frighteners on you because you are testifying against him, wasn't he?"

"Who told you that?"

"Your cousin Conn."

"You spoke to that Irish weasel? When?"

"Last night at your cottage." Stretch lowered his voice, and juggled his pen and notebook so he could extract a roll of fresh mints from his pocket, which he offered and James waved off. "Interesting carpet, by the way."

James squeezed his eyes shut for a moment. "You saw the green paw-prints then?"

"What green paw-prints?" Sergeant Stretch popped a mint in his mouth and started sucking. "I'm talking about the green streaks. It'a a pattern I haven't seen before."

"Green streaks?" James gave him a puzzled look, then the penny dropped. "Oh, don't tell me! Sooner you do something about *Taylor's Takeaway* selling anything other than Chico Rolls, the better! I trust the bottle I gave you is helping build evidence against them."

Sergeant Stretch switched back to his official voice. "You only gave it to me yesterday, sir. It's gone to the police lab where I am sure it is assisting with our enquiries."

Sergeant Stretch poised his pen. "Perhaps you can tell me why you didn't tell me Messerschmitt was standing in your garden each night."

"I didn't, um, think it was relevant."

"Not relevant? From what I've determined you were probably the last person to see him."

"Good heavens! Am I a suspect in his death?"

Stretch examined James's face and his next words came out slowly. "What is it you're not telling me, sir? I had assumed he'd done a runner before he could be dragged to his trial."

"Of course." James did an Oodles and rapped the side of his head with a knuckle. "That's a much more logical explanation. Don't mind me. I've seen too many reruns of *Homicide*."

Sergeant Stretch continued staring blankly at him.

"Oh, of course, you're too young to remember *Homicide* on TV? People died in every episode. But you're right. Why would Messerschmitt be dead? He's obviously gone into hiding to avoid the trial."

"Perhaps?" Sergeant Stretch stroked his long chin. "But what I can't work out is what dissuaded him from his tactic of trying to intimidate you. Or did he succeed in persuading you to change your testimony?"

"What are you implying? He never came close enough to me to engage me in conversation."

"And why do you think that was, sir?"

James shrugged. "These new rules about social-distancing couldn't be helping him do his best work. Even an ape like Messerschmitt would struggle to punch me from so far away."

Stretch gave him a look that said: *are you serious?*

"Oh, sorry." James looked down at Stretch's shiny size 18s. "Old habits. Sarcasm was one of my stock defensive tools when I was in politics. Truth is, I really don't know why he suddenly disappeared. It was nothing to do with me though. Gus hazarded a guess he may have come across a bottle of the bogus gin."

"Gus?"

"Gus Foot, our postman."

"Postie? Last I heard he was posing as a dodgy financial advisor."

"I thought he was legitimate?"

Sergeant Stretch squinted. "Don't you believe it. Ever seen him roll up his sleeves? Just because you can't see his bikie tattoos, doesn't mean they're not there. We keep an eye on him because we know he still has underworld connections."

"You watch him, do you? You seemed surprised to learn he had become a postman!"

Sergeant Stretch's squint intensified. "These are difficult times, Mr Northan. We *do* have a long reach, but the long arm of the law can't be everywhere."

————

When James returned inside, Wish-Wash and Oodles were sitting as far apart on the table as it was possible to be.

"Ask Oodles to pass me the butter," Wish-Wash said as soon as he had sat back down.

"Tell Wish-Wash to go to buggery," Oodles said. "If he wants to clog his arteries so badly, he can reach over and get the butter himself."

James sighed. "Are you two going to continue this cold war for our last three weeks of confinement?"

"Did you send Awesome Sauce packing, old son?" Oodles said.

"It wasn't him. It was Sergeant Stretch."

Oodles threw a hand to his forehead. "They're on to me, I told you."

"Relax," James said. "It was me he wanted this time. I wish I had never let slip that Messerschmitt was missing."

"What did you tell him?" Oodles said.

"What could I tell him? I don't know where that gorilla has gone." He leaned into his hand, which was resting on his elbow. "I've changed my mind. I think I will go sit by the mailbox and wait for Gus. He might know something."

Oodles glanced up at the clock on the wall. "Bit early, isn't it? Isn't Maddie expecting you to call? You need to order your lady-boy."

"What are you talking about?" James rose wearily. "Besides, Maddie can pencil me in another time. I don't want to miss Gus. I'll take a chair out there, and sit and read."

THIRTY-NINE
WISH-WASH'S SHOCK

G<small>US</small> <small>ARRIVED JUST BEFORE LUNCH.</small>

By then, James had only managed to read 3 per cent of *Ulysses* by James Joyce, but he had read all the pages several dozen times, such was his problem concentrating.

Gus flipped open his visor. "Were you waiting out here for me, Jimbo? About fucking time!"

"Why are you so gruff? I'm the one who should be worried. Messerschmitt is still missing," James said.

"That's because he's dead," Gus muttered over the low grumble of his idling motorbike.

"Dead?"

"Yes, that what I said. Nice to know your hearing aids are working, even if the beard you're trying to grow isn't."

James looked at the ground, then looked up again. "How did he die?"

Gus shrugged. "They didn't tell. I didn't ask. That's the way it works. All I know is you owe the hitmen $11,000."

"$11,000?" James hissed. "I never authorised that to happen; and, besides, you said it would only cost $10,000."

Gus turned off the bike. "You don't want to argue with these guys, Jimbo. It's your own stupid fault you've incurred a late fee."

Both their heads turned when a big silver car came up the hill and parked just behind them.

A middle-aged man in a three-piece pinstripe suit and carrying a leather briefcase got out from behind the wheel of the late-model silver Rolls-Royce Phantom.

"Cedric!" James greeted him with a nod of his head. "You've come personally. I didn't think regional travel was allowed yet?"

"Haven't you been listening to the news? We're allowed to go further afield now. It was actually nice to go for a long drive after all this time."

James beckoned him from the other side of the gate. "Come through. You'll find him inside."

Mr Rolls-Royce trotted down the path, and knocked on the door.

Gus eyeballed James. "What does that bloke want?"

"I have no idea."

They could see now Wish-Wash had answered the door and the two men were speaking.

"You knew his fucking name!" Gus said.

"If you must know, he's my silk from Hobart."

Gus sized up the man at the door. "Really? He looks too big to be a jockey."

"Not that kind of silk! He's a lawyer who's taken silk. A Queen's Counsel."

Gus looked around at the car. "Do you know how much these things cost? Strewth! I bet he charges like a wounded bull."

"He's not cheap, you're right. But he is the best."

"Why's he talking to Wishy, not you?"

"How do I know? I'm not his only client."

"But you said *he's* inside, which suggests to me you knew who he had come to see."

"All I knew was it wasn't me — so it must be either Bert or Clarence. *Both* of them are inside."

Gus studied his face. "Something's going on, isn't it?"

"If I were you, I'd be more worried how I was going to resolve this Messerschmitt mess."

"It's not my mess, Jimbo. You shouldn't have entered into preliminary discussions if you weren't going to accept the consequences."

"But I never gave my final approval!" James yelled.

Gus shrugged. "Who are you going to whinge to? The hitman ombudsman?"

"This is your mistake, surely?"

"What can I say? Miscommunications happen. But what's the big deal? Your problem has gone away. We both know you can afford it, even with the late fee."

"It's the principle of the thing."

"I think you'll find the blokes you're dealing with don't play well with principles. You were worried about one large man with a baseball bat standing outside, I'd be more worried about two larger men with baseball bats coming inside."

"They wouldn't dare," James hissed.

"Oh, wouldn't they? You should ask Oodles about the time he broke his leg? Then double the expectation of pain."

"Can't you tell them it was all a mistake?"

"And what then? Get them to put Humpty Dumpty together again?"

James closed his eyes to think.

There had to be a way out of this.

He opened his eyes to see Gus's stare still boring into him.

"You do know, Gus, that Sergeant Stretch is watching you."

The postman looked around, searching trees and telegraph poles for signs of movement. When that drew a blank, he said: "Is that the best you can come up with?"

"I wouldn't even use your phone, if I were you, because it's probably bugged."

"Are we talking about the same bloke?" Gus said. "Stretch is probably still trying to work out which button in his car makes his siren work."

"Be it on your own head if you want to be complacent. Don't say I didn't warn you."

Mr Rolls-Royce returned down the path. "Goodness, you never told me he has pink hair!" He got back into the car and they watched him wheel around the cul-de-sac and disappear down the hill.

Gus turned his bike back on and revved his engine. "Don't say I didn't warn you, Jimbo," he shouted. "Their late fee goes up $1000 every week so it could become quite expensive for you if you want to keep all your bones intact."

————

Wish-Wash was sitting at the yellow table with his head buried in his hands when James returned inside.

Oodles was sitting across the room in his armchair. "Don't ask me," he said when James looked at him for an explanation. "He's not talking to me. All I know is whoever came to the door has upset him big time."

James walked over and touched Wish-Wash on the shoulder. "What on earth is the matter, Bert?"

Wish-Wash raised his head. "He's nothing but a dirty, rotten mongrel bastard."

"Who is?

"The toff who came to the door."

"Who was he?"

"I didn't catch his name. He's some big-knob lawyer Marta has engaged."

"Marta?"

"Marta Kretocek. He says she's back from Poland."

"Your old flame?"

"Yes, he says she's filing for paternity back-payment for what she spent while she was bringing up Billy. Tucker, clothing, education. The flamin' lot!"

James gasped. "Can she do that? Billy Gumboots is dead. How can they even prove you were even his father?"

"That's what I told that ponce. And that's when he took mongrel bastardry to a new level."

"What do you mean?"

"He said they'd have no choice then but apply to exhume his body and do some DNA testing."

"Can they do that?"

"You know they can. If they can prove by DNA testing you're related to Conn, I'm going to be up for a lot of money I haven't got."

FORTY
X MARKS THE SPOT
TWO WEEKS TO GO

Oodles ran his calloused left hand along the fresh green paint on the armrest. "You've done a good job here."

Wish-Wash beamed. "Thanks, cobber."

The three old men were back sitting on the bench at the top of the garden, enjoying the first spell of good weather in a week. The days weren't normally this pleasant in the midwinter of June.

Oodles sat on one end, Wish-Wash at the other, James was sandwiched between them with two different arms wrapped around his back and his own arms trapped by his sides. He could barely breathe, and the urge to scratch his itchy bewhiskered face was driving him crazy.

How had it come to this again? A week ago Oodles and Wish-Wash were barely talking.

But they had found common ground in their different adversities, which had brought them together again.

Wish-Wash stretched his outside arm towards the winter sun, and yawned. "Are you blokes excited that in two weeks today we'll be free men again?"

Oodles flicked his head. "The only change for me, old son, is I'll get rid of you two, but I'll still be here. Shame about the cracked TV, but them's the breaks." He laughed to himself, then looked sideways. "Get it? The breaks?"

"Did I tell you I'm moving back into the flat above the museum?" Wish-Wash said. "Moose is going bush for six weeks, so it'll just be Awesome Sauce and me for a bit." He turned his head. "I suppose you'll be moving back into your cottage, Jimbo? What are you going to do if Messerschmitt reappears?"

"Lord knows!" James squeaked. He barely had enough air in his lungs to talk, let alone bellow. He was now certain Messerschmitt wasn't coming back. But he wasn't about to share that with the other old men. He hoped that they'd soon come to the conclusion the thug must have died of hand-sanitiser poisoning.

This still left the problem of Conn. James would just have to move him into the spare bedroom so he could take possession of the master en suite again.

James had another urge to scratch his face.

How come Wish-Wash never seemed to itch? The big man had a healthy facial growth again, yet it had only been a week since he had clogged James's last razor-blade.

Anyone else might have felt guilty he had ruined another man's razor.

But not Wish-Wash. He just lumbered along as if it were part of the universe's mysteries he couldn't explain, so why bother distracting himself from everyday life by worrying.

James couldn't see a way to resume shaving anyway.

Even if he asked Maddie to buy him new razor cartridges (which would be an awkward conversation since she probably assumed he was still using the electric razor), he would find it nigh impossible to hold a steady hand over the lather when he was so sick with worry.

Wish-Wash released his arm from behind James's back and shook it to get his circulation back. "Sorry about that cracked TV, cobber. If you want, I could come back and help you paint the 'X's on the road."

Oodles glanced sharply sideways. "What blinking 'X's?"

"You'll be needing them to stop the pilgrims standing too close together when they line up. You don't want them to go breaking the social-distancing rules."

"I thought you were only kidding about the Virgin Mary's crack?"

"Never more serious." Wish-Wash stood up, his faded Hawaiian shirt and orange-and-swirly-green tracky-dackies flapping in the gentle breeze. "Matter of fact, why wait? I'll get cracking with the 'X's now."

James shifted to the end of the bench, sucked in a lungful of air, and started scratching his face.

Wish-Wash held out his hand to Oodles. "Can I have the keys to the garage?"

Oodles frowned. "Why?"

"So I can get the paint."

The intensity in Oodles's voice rose. "You're not allowed to go outside the blinking front gate. And even if you were, I don't want a line of crooked 'X's up the hill. People would dig up the road looking for treasure." He locked eyes with James, and laughed. "Or bodies?"

James laughed nervously. Oodles didn't know how close to the bone that really was.

"What makes you think my 'X's would be crooked?" Wish-Wash asked. "Only a few minutes ago you were commending me for my excellent work painting the bench."

James rolled his eyes. Give him strength! Anyone would think Wish-Wash had painted the Sydney Harbour Bridge on his own!

He now knew though Oodles's renewed trust in Wish-Wash wasn't strong enough for him to confess he had relocated all the stolen paint.

Even if he thought Stretch had bought his denial, in the back of his mind he probably still wondered if Wish-Wash had been the one who had dobbed him in.

Oodles knocked a knuckle against the side of his head. "I've got no idea where the garage key even is."

FORTY-ONE
ICE-CREAMS AND EVIDENCE

WISH-WASH WAS first to see the man in the rainbow-coloured surgical mask come around the corner of the house.

"Tom? What are you doing here?"

"Sorry, I didn't mean to startle you." Tom Vance, the Windy Mountain council-clerk, was also wearing surgical gloves. In one hand he held a pocketknife with a red handle, and the fingers of the other hand were wrapped around a jar with a yellow label.

When he looked down and saw Oodles sitting on the bench, the cotton fabric of the mask went in and out as he spoke: "You're looking a lot better than the last time I saw you. When was that? 18 months ago?"

"Oh, it hasn't been that long." Oodles kicked up his left leg to show it was now in working order. "I'm sure you saw me in the street after I got out of hospital."

"I was with him, remember?" Wish-Wash said, his chest swelling. "But it wasn't in the street. I think it was in the Wind Tunnel Cafe."

Tom Vance studied him. "You've dyed your hair pink, Wish-Wash? Interesting."

"Bert is just an attention-seeker, Tom," James said. "You must know that by now? And don't be fooled by Clarence pretending his leg is fine now. If Dr Jenkins knew he was not using his walking stick, he would have conniptions."

Tom glared down at him. James imagined he was baring his teeth behind that mask.

Tom was a Rottweiler who thought part of his role was to manage the Mayor day to day. Thus, he tried to keep James away from his own daughter on the pretext she was too busy with the work of council. It must have irked him they now had daily phone contact.

James had liked the sound of the man before he had arrived about two years ago.

Tom Vance had served in the Australian Army, rising to the rank of sergeant and serving as a medic in the Timor conflict.

It was only after he arrived, however, he showed his true stripes. Rainbow strands of red, orange, yellow, green, blue and violet.

James had nothing at all against gay people. But Windy Mountain already had two home-grown homosexuals: the former deputy mayor, Peter Rowbottom, and the former dog-catcher, Doggie Dougall, who had come out of the kennel/closet to live with Rowbottom. For goodness sake, if they kept importing queers at this rate how long would it be before they demanded their own float in the town's Christmas parade?

When Oodles had broken his leg up on Bing Bong Mountain while fly-fishing, it was Tom who had come to his rescue. So, at least he wasn't completely useless.

"You never answered Bert's question, Tom?" James said. "What are you doing here?"

Tom squinted at him again. "Going for the Huckleberry Finn look with those overalls, are you, Mr Northan? I'm not sure about the wispy beard. A straw hat might help."

Before James could answer, Wish-Wash waved for shush. "Listen? Can you hear that?"

Oodles cocked his ear, and broke into a smile. "You know? You're right, old son. I can hear jingling bells now and they sound like they are getting closer."

The lines in Tom's forehead crinkled. "You blokes wouldn't know about the new ice-cream van?"

"Really?" Oodles said. "Someone's started a Mr Whippy round? In Windy Mountain? In winter? During a pandemic?"

"Yes, Bumface's sister has."

"Who?" James said, frowning.

"You know. Peter Rowbottom's sister." Tom looked up to the sky for help. "I can picture her but I can't put a name to the face."

"It's Daisy." James shifted uncomfortably in his seat.

"That's her. Daisy. I assumed she had dyed her hair pink to help promote her strawberry sundaes." He turned and surveyed Wish-Wash. "Your hairdo has me all confused."

"Are you sure it's her?" James said. "Last I knew, she was working as a volunteer at the hospital. Besides, how on earth would she come up with the investment capital?"

The jingle was getting very close now.

"I think they had to let her go," Tom said. "The hospital didn't get the surge of patients it anticipated."

"Where did she get the blinking van from?" Oodles said.

"I heard the hospital sold the old ambulance to Daisy for mate's rates."

James started spluttering. "That's preposterous. We paid a lot of money for that ambulance."

Oodles shrugged. "Probably about time they upgraded it. Good thing they never got rid of the drop-down window at the side."

"No way am I eating a soft-serve from the back of that vehicle!" James said. "The last time it was an ice-cream van people hadn't died in the back. "

The jingle seemed to be coming up the hill now.

Wish-Wash reached out to take the jar and pocketknife from Tom. "Me and Oodles aren't fussy." He turned to Oodles. "Are we, cobber?" He turned back to the council clerk and pointed towards the cul-de-sac. "Quick, Tom. Tell Daisy we want two double cones, choc-dipped with nuts and a chocolate flake."

Wish-Wash examined the ice-cream Tom had handed him, then flicked his gaze to the one Oodles was holding.

"They're exactly the same," the council-clerk said, puffing, before bending over.

"I beg to differ, cobber," Wish-Wash said. "Where's my stick of chocolate flake?"

Tom rose back to a standing position and looked at the ice-cream.

"It was there when I bought it." Tom mopped his sweaty brow with his handkerchief. "It must have fallen off when it brushed against an overhanging shrub when I was running up the hill."

Wish-Wash licked the side of his cone to stop melting ice-cream from dripping down the sides, then smacked his lips. "But the van came right up the cul-de-sac?"

Tom wiped his brow. "I was too slow getting out there. I had to run down the hill after it, and I didn't catch up to it for six streets. I had it in my sights three times, but each time it pulled away as I was closing in."

Wish-Wash started munching furiously. Anyone would think he hadn't eaten for a week. "I did wonder what was taking you so flamin' long. Good thing you had all that army training!"

"We didn't do a whole lot of chasing-ice-cream-van training at Duntroon."

"You should thank me then for opening up a new chapter in your life," Wish-Wash said.

Tom jangled the change in his pocket. "Anyway, that's $14 you owe me."

Wish-Wash's smile disappeared. "That's a bit bloody rich."

"Not really, it's only $7 each. You were the one who wanted doubles with all the trimmings."

"You never told me they'd cost that much." Wish-Wash waved a finger at James. "Not all of us are loaded to the gills like him. Oodles and me are proper pensioners. You should have asked for the concession."

"Don't you listen to him, Tom," James said. "Bert has a short memory when it comes to money slipping through his fingers. And why would Daisy even offer a concession? She's not running a charity van."

"So true," Tom said. "You've got to commend her for even trying to start a business in this environment, even if Taylor's Takeaway is putting up most of the money."

All three old blokes looked at him.

When Tom realised they had all locked in on him, he said: "That's what Daisy just told me. She said she couldn't have done it without Dave Jenkins's entrepreneurial spirit."

James looked from one muncher to the other. "I wouldn't eat those ice-creams if I were you."

It was too late. Oodles and Wish-Wash were well into their cones.

"Tastes all right to me." Wish-Wash upended the last bit of cone into his mouth, a bit like a seal doing tricks, then wiped his lips with a hand. "Not gin-flavoured, not hand-sanitiser, just vanilla ice-cream, chocolate and nuts." He licked the fingers and thumb on his right hand. "No chocolate flake though." He glared at the council-clerk. "But we can't blame Dave for that, can we?"

"For what it's worth, I think the police should get off his back," Tom said. "The only people who don't make mistakes are people who do nothing. Dave's having a go in a time of great difficulty."

James blew out his cheeks. "You think things are that tough? Spare me!"

Tom glowered at him. "You only have to listen to the news, Mr Northan, to realise we're in a ton of shit."

"The only radio we have here is stuck on one channel that has a different interpretation than me on what constitutes news." James looked daggers at Oodles.

Wish-Wash waved his hands. "You were the one who didn't want me to get Awesome Sauce in to fix it."

"Is that Texan kid still living in town?" Tom whistled. "He's not going home in a hurry now, is he? And who can blame him if he wants to stay? The U.S. is in this much deeper than we are."

"The U.S.?" James frowned. "Really?"

"You really don't get much news, do you? Is your telly on the blink, too?"

"You don't want to know."

"I can tell you Trump's wall didn't work too well keeping the virus out of the US. It arrived on planes and cruise ships, same as it did everywhere else."

"But everything seems to be getting back to normal in Windy Mountain from what we hear?" James said.

"It's not too bad in Tasmania now. That stretch of water that divides us from the mainland has been a disadvantage for a long time, but it's turned into a strength. We're isolated."

Wish-Wash pointed to the pocketknife and the empty Vegemite jar on the bench. "So, why are you here, Tom?"

"Oh that! Yes, well . . . " He turned to face Oodles. "I-I've been instructed to take some paint scrapings from your weatherboards so we can compare them with historic ones we've collected from elsewhere."

FORTY-TWO
'JUST DOING HIS JOB'

"He's nothing but a rotten mongrel bastard." Wish-Wash leaned on the wrought-iron fence and watched Tom drive off down the hill with the samples. "It's crook enough he dropped my chocolate flake, but vandalising the house goes beyond the pale."

Oodles, who was standing behind him, sighed. "He's just doing his job, old cock."

Wish-Wash swung around and looked hard at him. "His job? Aren't you flamin' worried?"

"You forget: Tom probably saved my life up on the mountain. He's unlikely to turn full circle and send me to the gallows now."

James pulled a face. "I wouldn't bet on it. It's not like the old days where a level of pilfering was tolerated."

Oodles laughed. "If you reckon they're going to put an old bloke like me in jail, you're dreaming. The public outcry would be deafening. Hasn't Maddie got an election coming up?"

"You leave my daughter out of this. I'm talking about the legal system, nothing to do with politics. Perhaps you'll get off with a large fine but believe me you're not going to get away with it."

"You don't think so? How are they even going to prove it so long after the event now I've hidden the evidence?"

"I think you'll find paint-flake testing is pretty accurate."

Wish-Wash frowned. "Jimbo is probably right there, cobber. If DNA testing can prove he's related to Conn, and that I'm Billy Gumboots's father, it'll probably be able to pin you to the wall."

James nodded at Oodles. "You forget, not many public buildings in the town escaped your green brush."

Oodles looked from face to face, and laughed again. "You're forgetting how long ago it all was. I reckon all of those structures have had second or even third coats by now. They're all probably a different colour entirely."

Wish-Wash waggled a finger. "The bench in the High Street still had some of the old paint."

"Ah, but it's not even in the town any more." Oodles turned around and smirked at James. "*Someone* let Manky Manning reassemble it in Slutz Plains and repaint it red."

Wish-Wash groaned. "Did you have to remind me? We haven't even got sitting together again in the High Street to look forward to after lockdown." He turned his finger so it now pointed to James. "Because of him!"

James raised his hands. "Will you chaps ever let bygones be bygones? Why would I want to relocate a bench dedicated to my own great, great, great grandfather anyway? It had nothing to do with me. Blame Messerschmitt. It was his idea."

"That's very convenient when he's not here to defend himself, old cock," Oodles said. "Did he go to boarding school with Manky Manning, too?"

"Show some respect," James screamed. "It's *Mayor* Maurice Manning."

"Can't you re-engage the old boy network to have the bench returned to the High Street, old cock?" Oodles said.

James was becoming hotter in the face. "Will you desist from calling me that?"

"What?"

"Old son, I can tolerate. But old cock is just vulgar."

Oodles stared blankly. "I call lots of people that. Old son, old mate, old cock. What's the difference?"

"I'm not old, so by definition neither is my, er, um, appendage."

"You are the cock-head who gave away our bench." Wish-Wash had flecks of white on his lips, possibly just leftover ice-cream.

James pinched the bridge of his nose. "Don't think I don't know what both of you are trying to do? You're trying to create a diversion!" He looked at Oodles. "It won't work. You did steal that paint, Clarence. Why don't you just own up?"

Oodles stuck out his jaw. "Let them prove it!"

"Please yourself." James lowered his voice. "But you're underestimating Tom Vance's tenacity. Those types of people can be very vindictive."

"Who the heck are *those* people, Jimbo?" Oodles said. "Council-clerks?"

"Homos."

Oodles raised an eyebrow. "You think Tom is bent? How did you come to that conclusion?"

"He told me himself."

"I've never seen any evidence of the sort." Oodles blew out his cheeks. "You don't think he was pulling your chain?"

"Why would he do that?"

Oodles folded his arms. "Oh, I don't know? He's probably pegged you as the town's biggest bigot, and is just having some fun with you."

"Fun?" James hissed. "He already has his fun at my expense every time I go to the council chambers to see Maddie. A man of my standing shouldn't have to take a number and wait in a queue. No telling what germs I might be exposed to sitting in that waiting room with him just on the other side of the counter. Never mind COVID-19, remember AIDS!"

Oodles unfolded his arms. "That's it then. I bet his plan is working. You've reduced your visits?"

"I bet he can't wait for our lockdown to end. It must drive him mad Maddie calls me every day. These people are control freaks, I tell you."

Oodles looked at Wish-Wash. "He's not listening to me, is he?"

Wish-Wash's eyes were already fixed on the man in the suit coming up the hill. "I reckon us two ought to go inside and let Conn try to talk some sense into the old cock-head."

FORTY-THREE
CONN TURNS UP

CONN TRIED to speak between gasps when he arrived at the gate but he might as well be spitting Gaelic.

"Say it, don't spray it, man." James took a white handkerchief out of his pocket, and dabbed his left cheek. "Where have you been anyway? You haven't been around for days!"

Conn broke into a smile. "So, were you worried about me?"

"Hardly. I've been more worried about not getting a status report on my carpets. Sergeant Stretch told me how Taylor's Takeaway had ruined them."

Conn frowned. "When were you talking to him?"

"A week ago, the day after he interviewed you at the cottage. Why did you have to tell him Messerschmitt had been standing in my garden?"

"Because he had been. You were terrified. He needed to know dat."

"That's the last thing he needed to know. His resources are already stretched to the limit trying to nail Taylor's Takeaway over the poisoned gin."

"Your nephew is still missing, by the way."

"Tell me something I don't know."

"Sergeant Stretch is exaggerating. Taylor's Takeaway didn't ruin your carpets. If anything, I like the green smudges because they remind me of home. I'm not too keen on the new holes though. But Adolf and Eva made those. I've never seen dogs trying to dig through the floor before."

James closed his eyes slowly. "Oh, this is worse than I thought. Damn dogs!"

When he opened his eyes, Conn was smiling. "Dat's the good news I bring, cousin. Happy days! I've banished the pair of dem to outside." He scratched his head. "Now I've just got to work out how to stop dem digging in the garden. It's like they're sinking little mine-shafts all over the place."

Conn glanced towards the shiny, green house. "What happened to your pals? I saw them here with you as I was coming up the hill."

"They've gone inside."

"Shame. I was hoping to be re-acquainted. They remember me from the pub in Donegal, right? I haven't met any of your friends, apart from Sergeant Stretch, Messerschmitt and Maddie."

"I wouldn't exactly call Clarence and Bert friends."

"Maybe it's for the best they're not out here because I know I'm not looking my sharpest." Conn tugged the lapel of his coat. "All of your suits are looking shabby, like."

"You've gone through the whole wardrobe!"

"I hear Taylor's Takeaway is now doing dry-cleaning."

The grunt of a motorbike engine coming up the hill made them turn their heads.

"Is dat the postman?" Conn said.

"Damn." James looked at his Rolex. "He's early."

Conn turned to go. "I'd better leave you to it. I'll call around tomorrow. Have a think about the dry-cleaning. I'd need to put it on your tab."

FORTY-FOUR
ANOTHER OFFER HE CAN'T REFUSE

GUS TUCKED his helmet under his arm and looked back down the footpath. "Who was that?"

"That . . . " James pointed to the back of the man walking down the hill. ". . . is my so-called cousin from Ireland."

"I thought he looked familiar." The motorbike's idling was soft. "He walks like you, he even dresses like you."

"That's because he's wearing my suits. He's also staying in my cottage, eating my food, watching my Netflix, and using my electricity and water. The end of this pandemic can't come soon enough if you ask me. He'll have no excuse not to go back to Ireland as soon as they reopen international flights."

Gus watched Conn turn the corner at the bottom of the hill, and disappear. "You don't have much luck with your relatives, do you? Which reminds me: you need to have a word to your son-in-law."

"Norman? What's he done?"

"He runs *The Pick of the Crop*, doesn't he? What's he doing running the same crossword puzzle two days in a row? I normally enjoy my sit-down in cubicle two, but there didn't seem much point this morning."

"Oh, that's why you're here early?"

James had been careful to avoid the postman all week. In his heart, he just hoped the whole Messerschmitt thing was a misunderstanding that would go away. His head, honed by years in political office, told him to keep a low profile though until the heat died down.

Gus reached into his mailbag and pulled out a letter.

James's eyes lit up as he reached out for it. "I don't believe it! He's not dead, after all! I never thought I'd be so happy to get a letter from Messerschmitt!"

Gus pulled the letter back. "Settle, petal. This letter is for Wishy. What on earth makes you think it's from Messerschmitt? Even if he has come back to life at the bottom of a mine-shaft, he still wouldn't even be able to write with the broken bones in his hands. All 27 of them in each hand!"

James gulped. "You're sure he's dead then."

"Why would they lie? These are honourable men. All they want is their $12,000 and you'll never hear from them again."

"$12,000!" James cried. "First it was $10,000. Then $11,000. Now $12,000."

Gus stroked his beard. "I told you. It's $1000 a week in late fees. I'm surprised you just haven't paid up."

"I don't even have the means of contacting them. I thought you were acting as a middleman, so I couldn't be connected to them and they couldn't be connected to me."

"I expect they'll come see you when they're ready."

James felt his eyes pop. "You gave them my address?"

"I had to, Jimbo, because I'm quite fond of my arms and legs. It's not healthy to argue with men like these."

"But I never even agreed to go ahead with it. You're the one who had the communication problem. I still can't see why you can't deal with it. I never wanted anything to do with the underworld; you grew up in it."

Gus continued stroking his beard. "I see your point, Jimbo." He turned and looked down the hill again. Conn was long gone, but James could see the pseudo postman had just had a brainwave.

"Would anyone miss that Irishman if he went away?" Gus asked.

"I certainly wouldn't! Good riddance if he wants to go off sightseeing."

"Hmm, the hitmen would probably cut you a good deal as a return customer. It would be a win-win. Your cousin would get to see a mine shaft on the West Coast, and no one here would even raise the alarm he was missing. It's almost the perfect crime. It'd still cost you a few extra bob but think of the money you'd be saving."

James snatched the letter out of Gus's hand. "I do not believe this! You are suggesting I order the execution of someone else in my family?"

Gus shrugged. "Personally, I'd have your crossword-fucking-up son-in-law next on the list, but you've got to go with your gut feeling when deciding who is the more immediate problem."

James was already a good way down the path when Gus started revving his engine.

James turned and waved the letter. "Don't even think about re-engaging them," he shouted.

———

He handed Wish-Wash the letter.

"What's this?" Wish-Wash had now hidden his hair under his brown and gold beanie, despite the living room being toasty warm.

"What do you think it is?"

Wish-Wash examined both sides. "It doesn't have a return address, but it does call me Mr Bertram Whish-Willson, so it must be from someone who doesn't know me very well."

"Why don't you just open it, and see?" James said.

"It might be a letter from the Tattslotto office," Oodles said. "Telling you you've won a lot of money."

Wish-Wash looked into the air. "Funny, I don't even remember buying a ticket."

He ripped the envelope open, unfolded the letter inside, held it close to his eyes and squinted.

"Well?" Oodles said. "What does it say?"

"I-I think it's some kind of invitation," Wish-Wash said.

"Oh, give it here," James said, ripping the paper out of his hands. Wish-Wash claimed he understood every word of the dreadful sci-fi novels he used to read, but the truth was he had dropped out of school early to become the town drunk. So his reading skills had to be questionable and, despite his protests, he really did need his reading glasses.

The first thing James noticed was the letterhead. It was from Cedric Billycock-Smythe, the lawyer who had visited in his Rolls-Royce.

It was indeed an invitation.

It was requesting Wish-Wash's attendance in the examination tent when Billy Gumboots's body was exhumed two days after they came out of lockdown.

FORTY-FIVE

YOU CAN'T WEAR A FOOTY BEANIE TO AN EXHUMATION

WISH-WASH WAS STILL SEETHING at breakfast. He sprayed milk and cereal as he pointed his spoon towards his pink hair.

"People will think I'm bloody disrespectful."

"You could always wear a hat to the exhumation," James said.

"I don't own a flamin' hat." Wish-Wash unloaded another Gatling-gun stream of coco-pops from his mouth.

James reached into his lap for his serviette and wiped his face. Why did the buffoon have to sit there?

Wish-Wash had arrived last at breakfast, dressed yet again in his blue singlet, and sat down on the chair directly opposite him.

"You do have a hat, old mate," Oodles said. "You could wear your knotted handkerchief hat."

"As if that will cover all my hair!"

"There's always your footy beanie. You could pull that right down."

This caused another eruption of coco-pops. "I'm not wearing a flamin' footy beanie inside that tent! Next you'll be suggesting I hold up a brown and gold banner for Billy to burst through."

"He was a football fan. You could say you were wearing the beanie in his honour."

"Billy didn't even barrack for Hawthorn!"

Oodles frowned. "Who did he go for?"

"Richmond."

"Ask Katie to order one from the Tigers' on-line merchandising store. They're not that expensive."

"What kind of turn-coat do you think I am?" Wish-Wash pretended to spit on the floor, though there was plenty of coco-pop evidence he already had. "I'm not wearing a Richmond beanie."

"You'd be doing it for Billy."

"Why? They haven't even done the DNA test yet. What if it shows he's not my son, after all? I'd be left looking like a total dick!"

"You're the one worried about your pink hair." Oodles turned sideways to James. "How are you sleeping, old son?"

James lifted a hand, which he tipped gently from side to side. "Oh, you know? So-so."

This was a lie. He had barely slept for nights. His chest just got tighter. He sweated profusely all night, even when it was cold. The loud beating of his heart kept him awake.

"I thought you'd be sleeping well now Messerschmitt seems to have gone?" Oodles said.

James smiled weakly.

He had gone to bed around 9pm and tried to read for a while.

Ulysses by James Joyce, ought to have been a good book for sending him to sleep.

In the space of a week, he had progressed to only 11 per cent of it on his e-reader. It was like riding a stationary exercise bike. No matter how hard he tried to read, he wasn't actually going anywhere. But it didn't send him off to sleep either. He kept thinking: what's wrong with me? This novel was highly rated by other intellectuals.

Last night had been no different to the previous night, the night before, the night before that . . .

He'd read the same page six times, then get out of bed and peer out the window.

Lack of sleep made the mind see all kinds of things.

One night he could have sworn Messerschmitt was standing in the shadows, pounding his baseball bat against his thigh. Then he worked out it was just a silhouette of Wish-Wash's trackies hanging upside-down on the rotary clothes-line and flapping gently in the breeze.

He only hoped tricks of the light would not fool him when the hitmen started sneaking up on the house. He couldn't mistake them for washing, could he?

Would they be brandishing guns? Knives? Baseball bats?

Would they give him one last chance to pay up the money owing? Or would they just leave him in a pool of blood as a message to anyone else who was tempted to renege.

When he got his imagination in check, he'd go back to his book and read the same page six times before finding himself at the window again.

And so the night progressed.

As James buttered his toast, he just knew Oodles was studying him, looking for tell-tale cracks. "Your eyes look bloodshot, old mate. Are you sure you slept OK?"

FORTY-SIX
NOW YOU SEE HIM, NOW YOU DON'T

THE DOORBELL RANG.

Ding-dong, ding-dong.

James raised a palm. "It's OK, I know who that is."

With his other hand, he resumed spooning marmalade on his toast.

Oodles looked towards the door anxiously. "Aren't you going to answer it?"

James took a bite of the toast, put it back down on his plate, and wiped his mouth with his napkin. "It's only Conn. He can just wait."

Ding-dong, ding-dong.

"You sure it's him, old son?" Oodles started to get up. "It might be important."

James pulled him back down with a sticky hand. "I know why he's here. He wants me to pay for his dry-cleaning bills."

Oodles looked at him. "Are you?"

"Certainly not." James picked up his toast again and examined it. "Especially not from Taylor's Takeaway. But it won't do him any harm to stand there on the doorstep wondering for a few minutes more what my answer will be."

"You don't think that's a cruel thing to do to your own cousin?" Oodles asked.

"I'm not made of money!"

"You could have fooled me." Wish-Wash raised his voice. "Poor Conn is stranded on the other side of the world with no money at all."

"I certainly didn't ask him to come here," James said. "I seem to remember you had something to do with that. Why didn't you ask him to stay with you? Instead, he's probably living higher on the hog than he's ever lived, and soiling my suits to boot."

"If it's your suits he's got dirty, I'd say you had a moral obligation to pay for the dry-cleaning," Wish-Wash said.

James opened his eyes wide as he glared across the table. "Who are you to lecture me on morality, Bert?"

"I've got my principles." Wish-Wash looked to Oodles for support. "Haven't I, cobber?"

"Oh, the paint thief is going to give the pink-haired lair a character reference, is he?" James said.

Ding-dong, ding-dong.

———

James still had his toast in his hand when he turned the knob.

A suit on a hangar was thrust at him as soon as he opened the door.

He reached out in a reflex action to catch it but let go of the toast as he did.

"Dave? What are you doing here?" He could see over the funeral director's shoulder the hearse was parked just beyond the fence.

"What do you think I'm doing?" Dave shouted, probably louder than any undertaker had ever raised his voice. "I'm returning your suit, you squealer."

James straightened the suit on the hangar. The lapels of the suit were sticky with marmalade and when he stepped on something crunchy he looked down and saw broken bits of toast under his feet.

"But I thought you were going to keep the suit, for, you know . . ."

Dave Jenkins's scowl deepened. "You know where you can put that voucher. The paper will be no good for anything else."

"But I thought we had a deal?"

"You're the one who made it null and void when you went squealing to the police."

"I haven't been anywhere for nearly three months, least of all to the police station. Why would the law even be interested in the quality of your dry-cleaning services?"

"I'm not talking about your stupid suit. I'm talking about the gin bottle you handed in to Sergeant Stretch."

James tried his politician's bluff. "Who told you that?"

"He did. Sergeant Stretch came to see me yesterday morning. He said you had given him the evidence that was going to send me to prison."

James scoffed. "Last I heard that bottle still hadn't come back from the police lab."

"Yeah, well, he seemed pretty confident the results would be damning for me." Jenkins tugged at the few tufts of hair left on his balding head. "We had thought we were in the clear. Every bottle had been recalled. Except one." He poked James's chest. "And. You. Had. It!" He kept poking. "And. Now. *He*. Has. It."

He had barely hung the suit in his wardrobe when the doorbell rang again.

Ding-dong, ding-dong.

It had to be the Irishman this time. Well, tough! He'd soon find out it was a wasted trek up the hill!

James walked down the hall and hovered behind the closed door, rehearsing in his mind what he was about to say.

Ding-dong, ding-dong.

Wish-Wash's raised voice came from the direction of the living room. "Are you going to answer the flamin' door, or not, Jimbo?"

James flung the door open.

Before he could talk, Sergeant Stretch handed him the bottle.

"Oh-oh, you're back?" James looked down at the gin bottle. "Why are you giving this to me?"

"I thought you'd want it back. It might be worth something for recycling."

"But don't you still need it to use as evidence in court?"

The policeman shook his head. "You didn't tell me you had washed away all the hand-sanitiser?"

"What?" He starred at the bottle. "Damn it! I should have known. Clarence rinses everything."

"It's left me looking like a goose. The whole case against Taylor's Takeaway has collapsed."

"But you haven't told Dave Jenkins?"

"How do you know that?"

"He was just here and he was furious."

Sergeant Stretch fixed his eyes on a spot above James's head. "So it was you he had just seen up here? I passed his hearse coming up the hill. I assumed someone must have died."

"Why did you have to tell him I was the one who gave you the bottle?"

Sergeant Stretch smiled. "I wanted to put the wind up him. I thought it would add weight if he knew the bottle had come from a former mayor and the father of the present mayor."

"I don't understand," James said. "Dave told me you were confident you now had enough evidence to send him to jail. How could you do that?"

"It's basic old-fashioned police work. Put the frighteners on until he folds and confesses."

"You don't think *old-fashioned* might be the operative word here?"

Sergeant Stretch gave him a hard look. "I went by the book. I did it exactly the way old Birty would have done it."

James rolled his eyes. "You should have learned from Sergeant

Birtwistle's mistakes. Learn to keep your overgrown feet on the ground instead of putting it in your mouth."

Stretch held out his thumb and forefinger. "I came this close to nailing that worm. How was I to know the bottle would come back positive?"

"Positive?" James looked down at the gin bottle again. "I thought you said it was negative?"

"It was positive to dishwashing liquid."

"When did you find all this out?"

"The bottle came back from the lab yesterday afternoon. But I decided to let Dave sweat a bit longer. You never know when someone might fold."

"Oh, good one. That's why he's just unloaded on me."

Sergeant Stretch frowned, then winked. "You can make a formal complaint if he threatened you. I'd be happy to follow it up."

"Oh, it was nothing like that. He's angry, that's all. You would have saved me a lot of grief if you had told him he was off the hook."

"Why would I do that?" Sergeant Stretch's Adam's apple bobbed like a boat in a storm as he spoke. "I know he's guilty, you know he's guilty, he knows he's guilty. It won't do him any harm to stew for a while. It'll make him think twice before breaking the law again."

"You're really the face of the new-age sensitive police force, Sergeant Stretch."

"What's that supposed to mean?"

"Think about it."

"You think I have time to think?" Sergeant Stretch raised his hand to the side of his head. "I'm up to my ears in work. We still haven't found Messerschmitt."

"I really can't help you any more with that. One day he was here, the next he wasn't."

"Do you know where I can find your cousin? I've got some follow-up questions for him, which might throw light on Messerschmitt's disappearance."

"Conn? He's at my cottage, I presume." He looked at his Rolex. "There's a good chance he's slept in."

"He wasn't there when I called yesterday afternoon."

"He couldn't have gone far. I don't think he's got much money. He's supposed to be seeing me here this morning. If he ever gets out of bed, I'll get him to give you a bell."

"So he has access to a phone?"

James raked his right hand down the side of his bristly cheek. He had forgotten about the landline. Lord knows how many calls Conn had made home to Ireland!

———

Conn never visited that day.

Nor the next.

Nor the next.

When Maddie complained during their daily phone call that both Messerschmitt and Conn had now vanished, and she had directed the council's new dog-catcher to remove the two German shepherds because they were chasing her cats around the garden, James knew he had to seek out the truth.

FORTY-SEVEN
MONEY WELL SPENT

JAMES WAS WAITING at the gate when Gus came up the hill the next day.

When the postman took off his helmet and gave his head a shake, James wished he had been standing further back.

"Do you mind?" He wiped his face dry with his handkerchief.

Gus smiled. "It's only sweat, Jimbo. You look like you could do with a hose-down. Even Wishy in his heyday never looked as haggard as you."

"Can you blame me for being a nervous wreck? First it was Messerschmitt, now my cousin Conn has gone missing. Did you have a hand in that, too?"

Gus dropped his voice. "You know I did. You waved the flag to start the process."

"I did nothing of the sort. All I waved was a letter to expressly forbid you from engaging those hitmen again."

"Really?" Gus frowned. "That wasn't a ready-set-go symbol? You should have said."

"If you hadn't been revving your motorbike like a hoon, you might have heard me."

"When did he go missing anyway?"

"The very same day!"

Gus smiled. "I told you these guys were good, Jimbo. They aren't bullshitting when they say they offer a same-day service."

James tugged his hair. "Is it too late to stop the process?"

"After four days? I doubt it. If it's any consolation, he probably got his wish to see another part of the state though."

James closed his eyes.

"I also got you a good deal, Jimbo. They've waived the late fee. So you're back to $10,000 per head."

James opened his eyes wide. "That's $20,000! All my money is tied up with investments."

"You'll just have to untie them. Don't feel bad about it. There has never been a better time to stimulate the economy." Gus tapped the helmet in his hands. "Do you think spring is coming early? It's getting hot under this, I tell you."

"Get a grip, man. It's only June!" James shouted.

"Why are you so angry? You blokes must be getting out soon?"

"Nine more days. Wednesday, the 1st of July after breakfast. Not that I'm counting."

"Just think. You'll now have your cottage to yourself. Money well spent, I'd say."

FORTY-EIGHT
WHAT'S SAID IN THE WARDROBE STAYS IN THE WARDROBE

HE WOKE up with a hand over his mouth.

James opened his eyes but it was so dark he couldn't even make out his assailant.

So it had come to this?

He had endured night after night of staying awake so the hitmen couldn't take him by surprise.

But they obviously had been playing the waiting game. They knew he had to doze off sometime. Exhaustion had finally got him. He hadn't even heard the window smashing. Or had they come through the front door? How had they known which bedroom was his? Maybe they hadn't. Maybe they had gone through the house systematically. Maybe Bert and Clarence were already dead?

"Shhhhh," came the voice from above. "Don't make a sound. We don't want to wake Wish-Wash."

Although he didn't have his hearing aids in, James could hear enough to recognise that voice.

What was Oodles doing in this bedroom?

"On the count of three, I'm going to release my hand. Ready? One, two, three . . ."

"It's you." James blurted when the hand was lifted.

"Who were you expecting, old mate? But I told you: you need to keep your voice down. We don't want to wake Wish-Wash."

"I don't understand."

"I can hear voices outside from my bedroom. What did I tell you? I've been dobbed into Crimestoppers, and we're being raided."

"What time is it?" James whispered.

"Quarter past one, give or take."

"Why don't you want to wake Bert? He might have some ideas."

"Are you kidding? I'm convinced now he was the one who dobbed me in."

"How could he point them to the contraband when he doesn't even know we moved it?"

"I'm trying to work that out. But why else would there be people out there crawling around in the garden?"

"Hmm." James swung his legs to the floor and saw in the moonlight flickering through the window that Oodles was wearing his woollen green tartan dressing gown.

This was very unfortunate timing. He felt confused.

What if the house was actually surrounded by the hitmen intent on breaking limbs or worse?

James sucked in a deep breath. "I suppose the time has come to tell you. These men in the garden might really be here to harm me."

James proceeded to confess all. Messerschmitt. Conn. The hitmen. The growing debt. The need to hide.

———

The wardrobe had standing room only. James was sandwiched between Oodles and the necktie Wish-Wash had given him for his birthday. He couldn't see the palm trees and naked lady in the darkness but the confined space smelt like a fish'n'chip shop.

He couldn't hear a sound outside because he hadn't had the clarity of thought to grab his hearing aids from beside the bed.

Sweat ran down his back, which was odd because he felt quite cold wearing just his pyjamas.

Oodles whispered he could hear Wish-Wash snoring. "Shouldn't we go wake him, too?"

"And blow our cover? Are you crazy?" James's muscles tightened and he wondered if Oodles could also hear his heart thumping.

"What if the hitmen go into that room and kill Wish-Wash by mistake?"

"That's a chance we'll just have to take."

When nothing actually happened in the next hour, and Oodles said he could still hear Wish-Wash snoring, James began to relax but he also began to regret he had even told Oodles about the hitmen. He knew now Clarence was right that they had actually come for the paint.

———

Oodles opened the wardrobe door a crack and the slither of light told them dawn had finally come.

"Do you think they've gone?" Oodles whispered.

"I hope so," James said.

Oodles pushed the door open and stepped into the room. He had his hand on his hip and moved with the fluidity of the Tin Man.

James followed him. Oh, his aching back!

Oodles cocked his ear. "Hear that?"

"No, I'll have to put in my hearing aids." James took them from his bedside table and fitted them into place, adjusting the volume with a squeal.

"Can you hear that now, old son?"

"No. I still can't hear anything."

"Exactly. We could hear Wish-Wash snoring last night. Do you . . . do you think he's d-dead. We ought to check on him."

"Oh, I don't think that's a good idea." The truth was James needed some sleep so he could get his excuses clear in his mind, and he didn't need Wish-Wash in his face yet. So he kept the lie going. "Bert's body might not be a pretty sight. Best to get some sleep before we go into that slaughterhouse of a room."

FORTY-NINE
THE MISSING BOOTY

WISH-WASH CAME through the living-room door about 8 o'clock, yawning and scratching his hairy belly.

James lifted his head from the table in time to see Wish-Wash release the bottom of his blue singlet.

"Strewth, you blokes look like something the cat dragged in," Wish-Wash said. "Were you sleeping?"

Oodles lifted his head and looked at the pink-haired man with his rheumy eyes. "You're alive!"

"That's what a good night's sleep does for you."

Oodles looked sideways at James. "I thought you said . . . "

James wished again he hadn't told Oodles about the hitmen. He eyeballed the big man and saw in his eyes he wanted some kind of explanation.

"We were hiding in my wardrobe all night, Bert."

Wish-Wash folded his arms and smiled. "Why?"

James said quickly: "We were hiding from Tom Vance's commandoes who raided underneath the house to seize the paint."

Oodles stared at James. "What happened to the hitmen?"

"Hitmen, Clarence? Squatting all night in the wardrobe has really done your head in. Do you need to lie down?"

"What are you talking about, old cock? You said the hitmen were going through the house systematically looking for you."

"Yes, I did tell you that, didn't I? I had to tell you that to keep you safe."

"But . . . "

James put on his politician's face again. "Goodness, did you really think I'd get mixed up with hitmen? Me? Check under the house if you don't believe me. I bet the whole stockpile of paint is gone."

"That's not what you blinking said last night. You said it was every man for himself. You were willing to sacrifice Wish-Wash."

Wish-Wash scowled. "I don't understand. How did the paint get from the garage to under the house?"

"Yes, well, Clarence and I decided to move it," James said.

"Without telling me?"

"He thought you might have been the one who informed on him," James said.

Wish-Wash swung around and looked at Oodles. "Is that true? You thought I was a dobber, cobber?"

"I can't lie, old son. But if those voices I heard *were* commandoes, that puts you in the clear." Oodles stroked his chin. "Only two people in the world knew where I had hidden that paint. And I didn't rat on myself, did I?"

Two sets of eyes fell on James.

———

Wish-Wash grabbed the flashlight from the kitchen, and went to check under the house.

When they heard the swing and clunk of the fly-screen door at the far end of the hall closing behind him, James started drumming his fingers on the table. "Even if the paint is gone, it doesn't mean I informed on you. Did you hear a dog out there last night? Dogs can probably be trained to sniff out paint."

"Why didn't you tell Wish-Wash about the money you owe to the hitman and the terrible things you had done to your own relatives?"

"Clarence, Clarence, Clarence. Can't you understand I made up that whole story to protect you? If you had suspected they had come for your paint, you would have gone out there to confront them. They might have had guns, it might have got nasty. You don't want to go down in local folklore. Three old men went into self-isolation but only two of them came out."

"Get away with you," Oodles said. "Why would Tom Vance shoot me?"

———

Wish-Wash returned shaking his head. "No paint tins stacked under there. I could see the imprints where they had been though."

Oodles turned to James, who was still sitting next to him at the table.

"Why are you looking at me like that?" James asked.

"You know why?"

"You still think it was me who told them where to look?"

"What would you think if you were me?"

"The sniffer dog is just one theory, Clarence. We might have been caught shifting it on satellite."

"In the blinking dark?"

"Ever heard of infra-red technology?"

"I'm also dirty that you ended any chance I had of stopping them. If you hadn't lied, I wouldn't have been hiding like a scaredy cat in the wardrobe."

Wish-Wash frowned.

Oodles turned to him and lowered his voice. "I'll tell you later, old son."

James leapt up from his seat. "Oh, no he won't." He eyeballed Oodles and waggled a finger. "What we say in the wardrobe, stays in the wardrobe."

FIFTY
COMMANDOES' SUCCESS
THE EVE OF LEAVING

James kept a low profile for the rest of the morning.

He stayed in his bedroom staring at his e-reader again and getting almost nowhere.

He left his sanctuary only to talk with Maddie on the phone. She confirmed the raid had happened overnight.

James could hear Oodles and Wish-Wash talking in the living room, so he spoke in an angry whisper. "I thought we had agreed for it to happen after I had left the house."

"I brought it forward on Tom's advice. He said the cloud cover was ideal."

"Do you know what difficulties this has caused me. Do you?"

"Sorry about that."

"But are you? This isn't more payback? I sent you to boarding school for your own good."

"Oh, Daddy. Not this again. It's been almost three months since I last thought about that. I assure you, I didn't mean to cause you trouble."

"It damn-well did."

"If it's any consolation, we got nearly 100 tins of paint back and Tom considered it a real delight to be able to call on old skills."

James returned to his bedroom to resume battle with *Ulysses*.

FIFTY-ONE
CAUGHT RED-HANDED

SOMEONE POUNDED on his bedroom door around lunchtime.

"Coming," James said.

"Make it snappy," Wish-Wash shouted back. "We've both got a bone to pick with you."

James opened the door a crack. "I thought you were calling me to lunch."

Wish-Wash snarled at him. "I didn't think anyone could top what Oodles has just told me. But I didn't count on talking to Gus Foot."

James opened the door wider. "Gus has been? Already?"

"He wasn't happy. He said Norm stuffed up the crossword again. It's thrown his whole day out of whack."

"He can't blame me for that." James's voice escalated. "If it had been up to me, I would never have let Norm marry into our family."

"That's the least of your worries, Jimbo. Gus has dropped you right in it." Wish-Wash pointed down the hallway to the living-room door. "Get out here. NOW!"

———

Oodles and Wish-Wash were sitting side-by-side at the table facing him as he came in the room.

James felt like he was coming before a judiciary. "I don't know what Gus has just told you, but do you really think you can trust him?"

"What do you think he told me?" Wish-Wash asked.

"Whatever it was, he's mischief-making," James said. "How on earth he got a respectable job is beyond me! He's always been a thug and a liar."

"Not to me." Oodles locked his fingers in front of him.

"Nor to me," Wish-Wash said.

"If he told you he'd engaged hitmen on my behalf, he's lying."

Wish-Wash frowned at Oodles.

Oodles squinted across the table. "Sounds like the same lie you told me in the wardrobe, Jimbo. How's that work? I've heard of villains synchronising stories, but never to *prove* their guilt."

Wish-Wash continued frowning. "Gus didn't mention any flamin' hitmen!"

James gulped. "He didn't?"

"No, all he said was you knew that high-falutin lawyer who sent me that letter."

James felt the blood leaving his face. "He did?"

"How much did it cost you to get a Queen's Counsel to drive his fancy car all this way to string me along and then follow up with a fancy letter? I can't even afford legal aid, and that's free."

———

"I was going to tell you both." James wrung his hands together and looked down at the yellow pattern of the table surface.

"Oh yes? When?" Wish-Wash asked.

"Tomorrow when we get out of here."

"You're nothing but a rotten mongrel bastard," Wish-Wash

shouted. "You think it's funny, do you? I was shitting bricks worrying about having to watch Billy being dug up."

"You two started this. I took it on the chin when you tried to fool me with that fake Tasmanian Tiger in the garden."

"Tried to?" Wish-Wash threw back his head and laughed. "You're all piss and wind, Jimbo! You swallowed it hook, line and sinker. If we hadn't put you out of your misery, you'd probably still believe it."

"Don't be ridiculous. You knew I would work it out. Why else would you own up so easily? I think you realised the scenario was just too far-fetched. Only fools like you two actually believe the Tasmanian Tiger still exists."

"Is that so?" Wish-Wash said. "Remember how you reacted when you saw the paw-prints in the paint spilled on the ground? You looked pretty flamin' convinced to me."

"Speaking of paint," Oodles said. "It was you who dobbed me in, wasn't it? I still can't believe you made that whole hitman thing up just to throw me! I'm in a whole world of trouble now."

"Of course you're not," James said. "You said it yourself. The council isn't going to worry about something that happened so long ago. Maddie isn't stupid. She knows pressing charges against an old man who was once a loyal servant would be electoral poison. Don't let anyone tell you she hasn't inherited my sense of humour though? I might have come up with the prank, but she was the one who made it all happen."

Oodles looked at him with tired eyes. "I can't believe you think this was the slightest bit funny, old cock."

"Oh, it's OK for you two to laugh about my jigsaw being messed up, smashing my new TV, discarding the fitness trackers Maddie gave you, laughing about the state of my beard, laughing about my brush with the fake Tasmanian Tiger and my kicking the bucket in the dark, and laughing about clogging up my last razor-blade cartridge with hair. But now the boot's on the other foot, you've lost your sense of humour!"

Oodles held his gaze. "But we'd never play cruel tricks like that on you."

James felt like a teenager banished to his bedroom without lunch.

It was his choice though. He wasn't going to let himself have to endure dark glares across the table.

They did call him for dinner.

"I'm not hungry," he shouted through the door.

"All the more pizza for us," Wish-Wash shouted back. "It's a bit like the Last Supper — the difference is Judas isn't going to be there this time."

James hated pizza anyway. It was peasant food.

But he had to bite his lip when the aroma started wafting into the room under the door.

That's when he realised Wish-Wash was torturing him. The pizza must have been on the other side at ground level. "Go away, Bert, and take that pizza box with you. I'm not interested."

As Wish-Wash's footsteps faded, James returned to his bed and his e-reader.

Every half-hour or so he got up and peered out the window, imagining how freedom would feel, how glad he'd be never to have to try to read *Ulysses* again.

He was so tired.

So, so very tired.

One last night! He just wanted to go home to his cottage and sleep for two weeks.

He switched off the light a bit after 9pm.

But he spent the next two hours tossing and turning and punching his pillow.

He finally got up and peered into the darkness out the window.

That's when he saw it.

A Tasmanian Tiger triggered the sensor light when it strolled across the lawn.

FIFTY-TWO
TWIST IN THE TAIL
FREEDOM DAY!

WISH-WASH RAPPED on the bedroom door about 8am. "Are you coming to our final breakfast or not, Jimbo?"

"Leave me alone."

"Your loss. Can I have your share of the golden syrup? Oodles is cooking pancakes."

"You know I don't eat that muck."

"You don't want to at least come out to say goodbye?"

"No! Go away!"

James held an ear up to the door and listened to the oaf's footsteps fading away. The smell of cooking pancakes started wafting down the hall. He had no doubt that Wish-Wash had left the living room door open with that exact outcome in mind.

He heard them both leave the house through the front door about an hour later.

Even then, he listened at the bedroom door for 20 more minutes in case one of them came back.

When he was confident he was truly alone, he changed out of the borrowed overalls and into his suit.

He picked up his bag.

He had imagined this day of liberation many times during his three months of self-isolation.

But he had never looked like this in his mind's eye — bearded, hungry, dressed in a damaged suit.

With any luck, he could just slip away quietly.

FIFTY-THREE
WELCOME BACK

He blinked against the light when he came out the front door.

He hadn't expected to hear any noise. So the din startled him.

Then his eyes adjusted to the light and he saw Sergeant Stretch waiting for him at the gate under a big sign that screamed WELCOME BACK Y'ALL.

He realised he was in the midst of some kind of street carnival set up at the top of the cul-de-sac. Where had all these people come from? He hadn't even heard the chimes of Daisy's ice-cream van driving up the hill.

He stood open-mouthed on the top step.

Maddie was standing next to Tom Vance in the near distance. She was dressed in a warm winter coat.

The quite pregnant Katy was leaning on the bonnet of the Tasmanian Tiger Museum ute talking to Joffa, Oodles and Wish-Wash. Awesome Sauce was standing on the back tray spinning a big wheel in front of a tower of tat. James could hear the click-click-click of the wheel spinning.

Moose Routley and Gus Foot were walking around selling tickets, dispensing change from their money belts. Didn't Gus have a job to go to? James couldn't see his motorbike.

The smell wafting from the Dagwood Dog van reminded James of the last time he had eaten six of these hot dogs in batter dipped in tomato sauce. It must have been at least 70 years ago at the district show. They had tasted a whole lot better going down than they did coming up — which had not endeared him to the other passengers on the shaking, whirly ride in sideshow alley.

The mystery deepened when he saw the backdrop of grey rain-clouds, which reminded him it wasn't even fete season.

He couldn't possibly know all these people.

That's when it dawned on him there was a good chance they'd know him though, and had just come to stickybeak. They were the same type of people who hung off every word of that God-awful celebrity radio, hoping for a mention of the Kardashians.

———

This was definitely not the way he had envisioned his release, but word had obviously got out and now he had no choice.

He stumbled down the path, and offered his coupled wrists to Sergeant Stretch.

"I'll go quietly," he said. "I'll confess. I just want to sleep again."

Sergeant Stretch stared at the proffered hands.

"Is it too late to get some breakfast at the jail?" James blubbered.

The puzzled policeman looked down on him. "Why are you so eager to go from one lockup to another? I only came to tell you we've found Messerschmitt."

James closed his eyes. "Don't tell me?" The last time he had felt like this was at his chess club when he realised he was about to be check-mated when he hadn't seen it coming. He had a hollow feeling in the pit of his stomach. He flicked through a gamut of emotions: anger, bewilderment, hopelessness, despair and regret. Why had he fallen into such an obvious trap? Hell and damnation! There wasn't a darn thing he could do about it. "Let me guess?" he cried. "You found him at the bottom of a mineshaft?"

"How did you know?" Sergeant Stretch sounded surprised. "Have you been speaking to that ratbag Gus Foot again?"

James opened his eyes to see Sergeant Stretch's inquisitive eyes bearing down on him.

"It was Gus who lined the job in the mine up for him," the policeman said.

James's eyes widened. "Messerschmitt is *alive*?"

"He thought he could lay low on the West Coast and avoid court. Thing is he didn't count on someone at his local pub ringing Crimestoppers, fearing he'd burn down that establishment next. Never get in the way of a man and his beer."

"But-but-but how did Gus Foot help him get that job?" James looked over to where the investment advisor/postman/former outlaw biker was still busy selling tickets. How could he?

Sergeant Stretch broke him out of his trance. "Do you want Messer-schmitt's version or Gus's version, sir?"

James turned his head and frowned.

"Gus says he has never even met Messerschmitt, which is a likely story — but I can't prove otherwise." Sergeant Stretch exhaled noisy. He stank of breath mints again. "According to Messerschmitt, Gus is actually an old mate who put him in touch with a mutual friend, who not only owns that particular mine but is also another character known to police."

The policeman pulled his notebook out of his pocket and turned pages until he found what he wanted. "Here it is. Bluey Brown." He stabbed the notebook with his index finger. "Apparently, he used to ride motorbikes when Gus Foot still went by the name of Foetus. Messerschmitt says Gus even paid his bus fare to the West Coast."

Sergeant Stretch scratched his head. "The problem is the absence of a feasible motive. I can't think what was in it for Gus."

James blinked at him. Now the checkmate had actually been deliv-ered, he knew he probably could help him with that information.

Though he had only ever gambled legally on the stock exchange, he'd wager money that Wish-Wash and Oodles had set him up.

But he couldn't say a darn thing about it to the policeman unless he wanted to incriminate himself in an intent-to-commit-murder charge.

Sergeant Stretch put away his notebook and exchanged it for car keys that jangled in his hand. "I just thought I should brave the cold so I could tell you as soon as you came out. Messerschmitt is locked in one of my cells now. Since he broke bail once, I very much doubt the do-gooder lawyers can secure his release again. That means you'll have the cottage to yourself again. I still can't work out where your Irish cousin has got to. Good luck there."

James watched him drive down the hill, then turned and looked skywards in despair.

He looked down again when he heard steps coming towards him.

It was Oodles and a beaming Wish-Wash, whose hair looked more vibrant than ever in this light — like he had dipped his head in a tub of pink fairy floss mix.

"Our little practical joke worked then?" Oodles slapped him on the back. "You must be pleased Messerschmitt is back in jail."

James hissed. "How could you do this to me? I haven't slept for days, I haven't eaten since early yesterday . . ."

"I'd say that's just a bit of payback for what you put us through," Oodles said. "The paint? The exhumation?"

James stamped his foot. "The difference is I confessed to both of those. You even hid in the wardrobe with me, Clarence, when you must have known the house couldn't possibly be surrounded by hitmen."

Oodles shrugged. "What else could I do? I couldn't give the game away." He exhaled loudly through his nose. "I knew fine well my cellar was being raided. But you know what? It wasn't the worst night I've ever had. I had my dressing-gown on. I knew you were the cold one and the frightened one."

He looked over at the house. "As I squatted in the wardrobe, I realised it wasn't the end of the world I was losing all my paint." He sighed. "I reckon the next time it needs painting, I'll be long gone anyway."

Wish-Wash slapped James on the back. "We *were* going to tell you, Jimbo."

"Oh, yes. When?"

"We told you about the pretend Tiger outside your window, didn't we?"

"We've been through this. You had to tell me about that before I worked it out for myself."

"Pig's arse. For your information, we only decided to let it go for fear you'd smell a rat. We knew this much bigger prank was brewing, and Oodles thought we might be laying it on too thick."

James rolled his eyes.

Wish-Wash smiled like a pink cat who had got the cream. "But now we don't have to tell you anything else, since Stretch has already told you."

"How can you possibly know what he told me?"

"We saw the look on your face after you made a fool of yourself. Everyone did." Wish-Wash pressed his wrists together and raised them. "*Handcuff me, take me in.* Seriously! And you reckon I watch too much American TV!"

Wish-Wash laughed. "Anyway, we had worked it out ourselves by that stage. Gus says Stretch had just put him through the wringer about Messerschmitt's reappearance. He denied everything, of course. He sends his regards, by the way. I hope you didn't drop him back in it."

"Do you think I'm a fool, man? If I did that, I'd be putting a noose around my own neck."

"I reckon you should relax then, Jimbo." Wish-Wash slapped his back once again. "We're square now, the three of us."

Wish-Wash pointed towards the gathering. "What do you think of the turn-out?" He pointed upwards. "Awesome Sauce painted that sign. Is there anything that boy can't do?"

"Since when has the word *y'all* been part of the English language?"

James pointed towards the young Texan on the back of the tray. "What on earth is he doing?"

"He's running a chocolate wheel, can't you see?" Wish-Wash put on his best spruiker's voice. *"Around and around it goes, where it stops nobody knows."*

"You jest!"

"No, it's another of Katy's clever ideas. Not only can you win boxes of chocolate, dinner-sets and toasters, the main prize is a year's pass to the Tasmanian Tiger Museum. The tickets are selling like hotcakes. Gus and Moose can't keep up with demand. Isn't that a piece of marketing genius?"

"I think I'd rather win the chocolates."

"I had forgotten how hungry you were, Jimbo," Wish-Wash said. "Tell you what? I'll shout you a Dagwood Dog to show we've got no hard feelings."

"No thanks. I-I've got a lot to fathom out. Where, for instance, has Conn got to?"

Wish-Wash was looking over his shoulder. "Speak of the devil. He can tell you himself."

James turned around to see his cousin trudging up the hill. When he came to a halt by the gate, he was wearing a shiny green suit James had never seen before.

"Sorry I'm late. I knew you were getting out today but the bus was running late. Finally, I get to meet your pals again." He nodded from face to face. "Long time, no see."

James frowned. "What bus?"

Conn surveyed the scene, then pointed towards one of the men selling tickets near the museum ute. "I thought dat fella would have told you. He said he knew you well."

"Moose?" James frowned.

"Is dat his name? Messerschmitt did call him someting like dat when he came to the cottage to take away your dining suite, but I didn't really catch it."

"Him? I thought you said it was a man with a truck."

Conn pointed to the Tasmanian Tiger Museum ute. "Well, what do you call dat!" He blew out his cheeks. "He didn't have dat big wheel on the back though. He barely had enough room on it for your dining suite."

James buried his head in his hands. "Do you know how much I had to pay for that table and chairs?" He dropped his hands and raised his voice. "Guess?"

"No idea," Conn said. "But yer man did say he'd get a good price for dem."

James felt the muscles tightening in his face. "He said that?"

"He came through with enough to pay for my trip to Hobart, anyway. I stayed in a hotel overlooking the waterfront. Spectacular views. Room service. Fluffy slippers. I even had money left over to do a trade-in for dis new suit." He brushed one side of his jacket. "Like it?"

James felt quite ill. Sweat beads had gathered on his forehead.

"Your man said he was glad to help you make sure I had a good holiday. So tanks for dat."

"I'll have both of their guts for garters?" James took a step towards the ute, but Oodles pulled him back. "Do you think that's a smart move, old mate, when you consider who's come off worse in your past confrontations?"

James turned and waved a finger at Oodles. "You'll get yours, Clarence. You and Bert were in cahoots with them. Don't expect me to forget that!"

"Calm down, Jimbo," Wish-Wash said, "What you need is something to help you cool down." He started walking towards the middle of the road but turned his head. "I'll be right back."

James felt another arm wrap around him. This time it was Conn, who drew him close.

"Can I have a word in private, cousin?" he whispered. "Only I noticed it when I was walking up the hill. Did you know you have a big hole in the back of dat jacket?"

When Wish-Wash returned he was carrying a brace of ice-creams in a cardboard carrier — three double cones with sprinkles and protruding chocolate flakes that sat on top like luscious brown sails.

"Strewth, old son, can you afford all that?" Oodles said.

"Daisy said they're on the house. She says we deserve them, especially Jimbo."

James didn't give it a second thought. He gulped his cone down even faster than Wish-Wash did.

FIFTY-FOUR
BLOKES ON THE MEND
A WEEK LATER

JAMES INSPECTED the back of his hand and winced at the dried blood from the cannula. "I can't believe I'm in this room again."

Maddie was sitting on the other side of his hospital bed. "It's your own fault, Daddy. You should never have scoffed down that soft-serve ice-cream."

"How was I to know it was going to give me food-poisoning?" He looked over at Wish-Wash in one of the other beds. "You have to take some of the blame for this, Pinkie."

"Me?" Wish-Wash looked across at Oodles, who was in the third bed. "That's not fair, is it cobber? Jimbo should probably be thanking us for saving his life. We had to stop him from overheating. I knew he wouldn't want Moose giving him mouth to mouth again."

"Oh, for goodness sake." James turned to Maddie and growled. "You're the mayor now. Can't you do anything about it?"

Maddie brushed a loose thread from her gown. "Do what exactly? Don't you think I have enough to worry about?"

James wriggled higher up on his pillows. "Look, we know Taylor's Takeaway is financially backing that ice-cream van."

His daughter's eyes widened. "So?"

"So they've got form when it comes to poisoning. The gin, remember?"

"Sergeant Stretch couldn't mount a case, you know that."

James glanced darkly at Oodles. "We can blame Mr Fairy Liquid for that. But it doesn't alter the fact that I wouldn't put it past Dave Jenkins to have sent Daisy up there with tainted ice-cream. On the house? Pull the other one!"

Wish Wash leaned over. "Sorry to interrupt, Jimbo, but I overheard the nurses talking and they say if you look out the window at night, and the light's just right, you can see a Tasmanian Tiger . . ."

―――――

The old men weren't always old. The next book in the Windy Mountain series steps back in time.

Discover how the tensions began.

BACK TO THE BEGINNING

BOOK 6 OF THE WINDY MOUNTAIN SERIES

This series actually started in 1993 when I wrote my first novel , then called *Apples*. There were no eBooks in those days, and no print-on-demand services. I reworked the novel for the digital world in 2017 and changed the title to *Who Knew Tasmanian Tigers Fat Apples!* I figure now is a good time for you to read the prequel before we go back to the future. **BUY IT**

Read an excerpt from Chapter 1

PERVERT OF INTEREST

Sergeant Randolph Birtwistle wished now he hadn't left the shelter of the bar at that precise time.

If he hadn't been trying to beat the rain, he wouldn't now be standing in front of the bench knowing full well who was sitting on the other side of that newspaper — but still feeling duty-bound to ask the question:

"Mr Mayor, is that you?"

Mayor James Northan lowered his rain-speckled newspaper. "So you *are* here, sergeant?"

Birty sighed. A few minutes earlier he had been warm and dry at the footy club, basking in the glory of a heart-stopping victory. But he had abandoned his glass of sarsaparilla when he saw dark clouds out the window of the bar.

It had been easier to make this 100-yard dash to the police station when he was younger and slimmer. The raindrops blurring his spectacles didn't make it any easier this afternoon.

It's a wonder he even noticed some idiot was sitting on the bench on the grassy verge in the middle of the High Street. But his reflexes got the better of him and he slid to a halt. By the time he took in the blue pin-stripe trousers, the shiny shoes and a masthead that told him the newspaper was *The Financial Review,* it was all too late.

"I've been trying to ring you all afternoon, sergeant." Even when Mayor Northan was looking up at him he made Birty feel he was looking down at him. "Has any progress been made on the missing telephone box?"

Mayor Northan didn't wait for a reply. "If you were more in touch with the community you'd know people use that phone box — old people especially."

When Birty sat down, the dampness seeped through the back of his pants. He closed his eyes and counted in his head . . . *one, two, three . . .* his missus had ironed these trousers! He sighed again. "You didn't get to the game?"

"I had better things to do." Mayor Northan stabbed a finger at the newspaper. "I found an interesting article on windsocks."

"More interesting than watching Windy Mountain win a place in the grand final? Moose Routley kicked the winning goal on the siren."

The Mayor curled his lip. "Oh, for heaven's sake! That means I'll have to talk to the players in front of half the town!"

"If it's any consolation, I don't think you'll have to talk to Moose. Silly bugger got himself reported for punching an opponent."

Birty stood and prised back his trousers. "Sorry, but I have to get going. This rain is getting heavier." He could see beads of water on the Mayor's nose now. "I really have to get to work for my very last Saturday night shift. Sooner I start—"

"I thought you had months to go?" Mayor Northan's eyes widened.

"No, only six more shifts. We're booked on a cruise in 10 days' time." Birty removed his spectacles and wiped them with a hanky. "Rita's been asking me to take her on a South Pacific holiday for years."

"Don't you think 60 is a bit young to be retiring? You're only three years older than me! You're not thinking about another career?"

Birty laughed as he put the glasses back on. "I'm planning on catching lots of trout."

"Pity. I could do with someone like you to help me with my new project." The Mayor lowered his voice. "What would you say if I told you I've decided not to sell my orchard after all?"

"I'd say that would make a lot of people around here very happy."

"Would it?" The Mayor smiled. "What I've decided to do now is hang on to the land, rip out the orchard and build a windsock factory on the site."

"How's *that* going to make things better?" Birty resumed his silent counting . . . *five, six, seven* . . . "That orchard is a part of the heritage of this town. People won't let you tear it down."

"I've obviously misjudged you, sergeant. You're allowing sentimentality to muddle your mind."

"Look, I've really gotta go, Mr Mayor. You'd better get some cover, too, before you catch your death." With that wishful thought, Birty crossed the road.

———

Birty heard Constable Smith and Junior Constable Stretch arrive about 6pm. Their boots squelched on the linoleum floor as they came down the hall.

Birty growled when he saw the trail of muddy footprints behind them when they came into the charge room. "I hope you young blokes haven't been drinking?"

"Of course not, sarge," Smithy said. "We only had a few lemonades to celebrate."

Birty tried to ratchet up his grumpy look so Smithy wouldn't be able to detect he shared his excitement. "Just as well I've decided to work one last Saturday, eh?"

"Thanks, sarge. I owe you."

"Just win the premiership. Then you can retire from the game on a high note."

Birty's mentors had schooled him in the art of tough love, which is how come he tried hard not to give the impression he thought much of the football skills of young Smithy.

He had to admit Smithy was a darn good ruckman. But he'd reached the same fork in the road Birty had come to 35 years earlier.

They had already had THE talk.

"You have to make up your mind." Birty tapped his index finger on Smithy's chest. "Do you want to hang with the boys every Saturday afternoon or do you want to further your career with the Police Force? Because. You. Can't. Do. Both."

Birty couldn't believe it was 1993 already. He had had his retirement date circled in his diary for years and now it was just about here. He had come to Windy Mountain nearly 40 years before as a junior constable. He had married a local girl and done his best to get involved in the community.

Most of the year Windy Mountain was a law-abiding little town, and Birty and Smithy didn't have to raise much of a sweat.

Except for the missing telephone box, and the frequent, but peaceful, locking up of The Big O, a copper's life around here was pretty quiet.

Smithy now had a new colleague. The idea was Smithy would step up to become station boss and Stretch would become his assistant. Stretch had never played football but Windy Mountain had already signed him for the next year on the thinking if he brought nothing else to the team at least he was big enough to get in his opponents' way. Birty wondered how long it would be before Smithy was thumping his finger on Stretch's chest during THE talk.

Then again, perhaps that would become a thing of the past. Policing had changed and he guessed it would continue to evolve. Birty remembered when it was quite acceptable for him to clip schoolboys under the ear if they were spotted smoking behind the change-room sheds at the Football Ground or caught nicking fruit from Northan's orchard. And everyone turned a blind eye if bully and petty thief Freddy Cuthbert was brought from the cells with a black eye.

All this political correctness and sticking to the rule book had been coming for years. Smithy would probably cope. But he was still going to have to hang up his boots at age 24.

Birty actually welcomed the arrival of the muddy boots. Mopping the floor would be a welcome break from trying to tidy up all his paperwork. That's another thing that bugged him these days. Were all these forms really necessary?

"You didn't see the Mayor across the road when you came in?" Birty said.

Smithy scoffed. "Are you joking? It's raining cats and dogs out there now!"

"You know the Mayor? He's so full of himself he probably thinks he can command the weather to change."

Smithy and Stretch wouldn't have heard him. They had turned around and were headed to the urn.

"Hey," Birty barked. "What do you think you're doing?"

"We're just making a drink, sarge."

"This isn't a blooming cafeteria! I want you two out on the street A.S.A.P. I don't want any over-zealous spectators thinking they can misbehave in this town."

Smithy looked at his watch. "You must have seen how many people were packed in the bar? If anyone's managed to cut through and order more than four beers by now, I'd be surprised. No one will be unruly at this hour, especially in this weather."

"Just do it, son, OK? When you've got your bum in this chair, you can do what you like. Right now . . ." He pointed to the mug beside him. It said in big letters: THE BOSS.

Smithy and Stretch put on their raincoats and went out. At 11pm they made their first arrest. But this one was expected on a Saturday night. They carried The Big O in and deposited him in the cell.

———

He was filling in the final minutes of his shift by trying to come up with a name for *The Pick Of The Crop's* cow when the front door slammed again.

Birty glanced up at the clock on the wall. It was nearly midnight.

The shouting and screaming and thump-thump-thumping noise was getting louder as it came up the corridor.

When Smithy came through the door to the charge room, he lowered his rain hood and smiled.

He was carrying a red apple and a yellow apple.

Trailing him was Stretch, who was handcuffed to a woman who was beating him with a handbag. She was as ugly as a hat full of arseholes.

Second thoughts, Birty realised it was actually a young man dressed in drag.

He was wearing thick makeup, a wig, a pink dress, green stockings and a pair of sand-shoes. Stretch was trying to shield his face with his free hand, but his shoulders and knuckles were taking a pounding.

The sergeant jumped to his feet. "Now stop that. I won't tolerate my constables being assaulted."

The man stopped in mid-wallop. "He called me a pervert."

"That's not correct, sarge," Smithy said. "We've gone by the book on this one, haven't we Stretch? We arrested this fellow riding a bicycle on the High Street."

He pulled a notebook out of his coat pocket and read from it in a monotone. "When the prisoner asked why he was being arrested, Junior Constable Stretch said he was *a person of interest*." He added, "Not a *pervert* of interest, sarge."

Birty scratched his head. Riding a bicycle while looking ugly wasn't actually a crime.

"Can we have a moment, Constable Smith?" Birty ushered Smithy to a corner where they turned their backs on the prisoner and Stretch.

"What was he doing wrong?" Birty whispered.

"He was dressed in women's clothing in public between the hours of sunset and sunrise. That's against the law in Tasmania."

Birty tugged at his dwindling strands of hair. He had booked drunks, traffic offenders, even a thief or two, but he had never had to deal with this type of thing.

He walked back over to the prisoner and eyed him up and down. He was about 5 foot 7.

"Take off that wig and let's get a proper look at you."

Birty felt a shower of water on his face as the wig came off. But before he could protest, he heard two thumps behind him. When he turned, Smithy looked stunned — as if he suddenly realised he knew this fellow. But he didn't say anything. He just stooped down to pick up the apples from the wooden floor.

"Sorry, sarge," he said when he stood back up. "Exhibit A and Exhibit B. He was wearing these inside his brassiere."

"For crying out loud." Now the prisoner was wig-less, Birty could see his short hair fell somewhere between blond and red-head. "You can't arrest me for stuffing apples down my front!"

"Don't start telling me what I can or can't do in my own police station," Birty said. "Don't you know it's against the law for men to wear women's clothes in public?"

"Between the hours of sunset and sunrise," Constable Smith added.

"I don't normally dress like this. I was riding my bike home from a football club fancy-dress party, trying to beat the rain squalls. It wasn't my fault my golden delicious fell out of my left cup. When I stopped to pick it up, these two blokes arrested me."

Birty eyed the prisoner up and down. "You're not from around here, are you son?"

"I come from Queensland. I live in Blackstump Road now."

Birty scratched his head. Blackstump Road was a few miles south-east of the town centre. The two run-down farmhouses along the road were now occupied by squatters.

Birty glanced at the clock again and it reminded him Rita had phoned 15 minutes before to say she was going to bed and was leaving his supper in the oven. It was drying up with every second.

So much for hoping for a nice quiet start to his final week in the job!

He went to the counter, opened the charge book, then picked up a pen. "OK, son, what's your name?"

"Les . . . Les Johnson. But everyone calls me Johnno. Why are you writing that down?"

"*I'm* asking the questions. Age?"

"Twenty-four."

Occupation?"

"I'm an assistant Tasmanian Tiger hunter." The prisoner craned his neck to see what the sergeant was writing.

Birty looked around and growled. "A what?"

"I'm helping Moose Routley to find Tasmanian Tigers."

"Moose Routley the footballer?"

"Same bloke."

"What's he doing searching for a dead animal?"

"He says there is a good chance it still lives."

"Does he just? I'd say he'd get better odds on beating that striking charge from today."

———

The sergeant walked ahead along the corridor. He unlocked the outer cell door, then stepped aside to let Smithy and Stretch go past with their prisoner.

He then squeezed by them and opened a steel door. "Hopefully a night in here will help you come to the conclusion your type is not welcome in this town. In you go . . . mind your head."

He pointed to somewhere in the gloom. "You'll find a clean blanket on that bed."

When they returned to the charge room, Smithy and Stretch walked over to the urn, but Birty called them back.

"You looked like you knew him, Smithy?"

"Only when he took off his wig, sarge. I've seen him around the footy club with Moose."

Birty scratched his head. "Did you know Moose was a Tasmanian Tiger hunter?"

He shook his head. "We assumed he was a hippy. Tiger even had to find him some boots so he could play."

———

Johnno pounded on the door and hollered through the peephole.

"Let me out . . . there's been a misunderstanding."

The next second, he jumped when someone pinched his bottom, and he nearly banged his head on the low sloping ceiling.

"What the . . . ?" He swung around with a swish of his dress. He couldn't see anyone. The room had a cold chill. The only illumination came from a low-watt lightbulb recessed into the ceiling, and he squinted into the semi-darkness. He could hear heavy breathing, and as his eyes adjusted he could make out a dark shape on one of the two beds, the one on the left. The shape's chest was rising up and down in time to light snoring. Or *pretend* snoring?

Johnno walked over and prodded the man in the ribs. "How do you like it? Not so funny now, is it?"

The man opened his eyes, gasped and sat bolt upright, blasting Johnno with alcohol fumes.

"Jesus, Mary, and Joseph." The man made the sign of the cross then covered his eyes. "A lady! Here!"

Johnno held up the wig. "Can't anyone tell the difference between a bloke and a sheila in this town?"

The man examined Johnno more closely as if he were trying to make out something in the fog.

"Oh, tank the Lord, you're a fella."

The man spoke with an Irish accent. He had at least one double chin — perhaps more, it was hard to tell in this dark room. He was bald but he had stubble on his face. He wore a khaki jumper and a pair of paint-speckled green and brown corduroy trousers with a rope for a belt. He swung his feet around and to the floor and eyed his new cell-mate up and down. "But . . . but . . . why are you wearing a dress?"

"It's a free world. I can wear what I like, can't I?"

"Well . . . no, not here . . . I tink Tasmania has a law prohibiting men from wearing dresses . . . Why did you wake me?"

"I roused you, mate, because somebody pinched me."

"Pinched you? Pinched you where?"

"You must already know that because you're the only one in here."

"I was sound asleep, I was, until you prodded me." He put out his hand. "I'm Father Ryan O'Shannessy."

"You're a priest?"

"Well, an EX-priest. Now I'm the town drunk. Everyone calls me The Big O."

Johnno shook the hand tentatively. "Say, you're not the bloke who saw a Tasmanian Tiger in the main street?"

"Noooo. Dat was one of my predecessors." He pointed to a long list of names gouged into the green paint that covered the brick walls. Johnno could just make it out at the top. *Wish-Wash, first guest of this cell, July 1965.*

"Someone told me this cell was used to house Irish convicts in the 1840s."

The drunk/priest laughed. "Far as I know I'm the only Irishman who's stayed here." He pointed again. "Dat's my name right under Brian Jacobs. He was a regular guest here, God rest his soul. Birty locked Brian up so often, it's a wonder he hasn't come back to haunt the place. Have you not run into Wish-Wash around the town? Big fella who wears loud clothes, laughs like a donkey?"

"No, but I'm only fairly new to the area. Why would someone pull my leg about the age of these cells?"

The Big O shook his head. "You sure you haven't met Wish-Wash? You can still see the ruins of the old convict cells near Northan's orchard. But I wouldn't go poking around dare in the dark — not unless you're happy to run into the ghost of Colonel Northan."

Johnno sat down on the side of his bed. He inspected the putrid blue cover and saw it encased a thin rubber mattress, which he lifted to reveal the concrete slab underneath.

"If it wasn't you who pinched me, who did?"

"You can see dare's nowhere for anyone to hide."

"Are you saying I imagined it?"

"All I'm saying is it wasn't me. Why would I do dat? I was sound asleep. The last ting I remember is being evicted from the bar at half-time of the footy and lying down somewhere."

Johnno folded his arms. The cell stank of urine, disinfectant and booze. His nose led his eyes to the stainless steel toilet in the corner. He looked up to a tiny window with bars high on the end wall, where the sloping ceiling was at its highest. He couldn't see the rain outside but he could hear it.

BUY IT

AUTHOR'S NOTE
WHO KNEW 2020 COULD BE SO FUNNY?

I WROTE *Blokes in the House* on the dining room table during lockdown. I had given up my normal working space to my wife, who had a real job.

Where I live escaped the worst of the pandemic, so restrictions were lighter in Canberra than other parts of the world.

Still, when a friend suggested I write a lockdown novel, my immediate instinct was "no way". How could I possibly find humour in it? We had already suffered through bushfires, a terrible hailstorm, now this.

I was halfway through another novel but that writing came to a grinding halt because I just couldn't concentrate with everything going on in my world.

But I had to do something!

I decided to embrace the lockdown idea after all.

But I adopted a different approach.

In the past, my novels have appeared fully formed.

This time I decided to release 12 chapters as I wrote them. I asked my cover artist, Maria Connors, to provide all the artwork I needed, and they dropped every few weeks with minimal editing.

I already had the characters I needed. They come from my Windy Mountain series. I threw the three oldest characters in a house together for three months and the story developed as I unravelled it, using cameos from other characters who had appeared in previous novels and finding humour in things I heard or read about. Towards the end, I knew exactly where the story was going. But in the beginning, this wasn't so much the case. The only thing I knew was the three old men would leave the house after three months.

At that stage, I stitched the 12 instalments together in one proper novel and made it the next book in the series.

I've tweaked them a bit, but not much. I corrected stuff, and added some clarification and some minor storylines, but the basics remain the same.

So this is the novel I never actually planned — a rare welcome gift from 2020!

Who knew that year could actually be funny?

I hope you enjoyed it.

TROUBLESHOOT FOR ME

This novel has been professionally edited. If you've got this far my guess is you've successfully navigated the Australian spelling, slang and deliberate oddities. But typos always manage to slip through the net, so by all means let me know if something's out of order.

– John Martin
https://johnmartin-author.blog

MY BOOKS

Windy Mountain series

Lie of the Tiger (#1)

He's not who he says he is. Who will rescue him?

———

Blokes on a Plane (#2)

Why is the mayor speaking old English? And where has he disappeared to?

———

Whitey and the Six Dwarfs (#3)

Troupe of Elvis impersonators come to the rescue.

———

Blokes in Donegal (#4)

Three old blokes go to Ireland hoping to discover family history. The mayor had to take his great, great, great grandfather's head, didn't he!

Blokes in the House (#5)

How the old blokes coped with COVID quarantine (clue: the major didn't).

_____

Who Knew Tasmanian Tigers Eat Apples. (#6)

Back to before the beginning. Wish-Wash leads a public revolt.

———

Who Knew Tiger Sharks also Eat Apples? (#7)

A character from the old days returns in an unlikely guise. It's all about comic revenge.

———

The Life and Deaths of Billy Gumboots (#8)

'His foot, my boot.'

———

Blokes Send in the Clones (#9)

Two old blokes have a crack at cloning a Tasmanian tiger.

To come:

10 — Blokes do the Block

Someone marries, someone dies. Might even be the same old bloke.

———

Funny Capers DownUnder series

The Wrong Magician (#1)

This time he has to make himself disappear.

———

Daddy's Great Escape (#2)

If Mad Bill hates people so much, why does he make it so hard for them to leave his island?

———

Escape from Mad Bill's Island (#3)

He came seeking to find out what the British were up to on the island in World War 2. He won't like the answer.

———

Major B.S. comes to the end of his Rope

It all started when he rescued the wrong group of people from a prisoner-of-war camp. It just becomes worse.

———

www.ingramcontent.com/pod-product-compliance
Lightning Source LLC
Chambersburg PA
CBHW020746250626
47155CB00003B/938